I AM SENDING A PRESENT TO MY MOTHER. IT WILL ARRIVE ON MAY 1ST FROM MY MOTHER'S SON.

"Yesterday was May 1st," said Rachel. "It's late."

She was like a child whose birthday had been overlooked.

"Either the card is honest, and my son is around. Or somebody hates me."

Next day the first body arrived, afloat in the river, but late for its appointment. It had got caught in the chains attached to a string of barges. This had delayed its transit up river. Otherwise the tide would have deposited it sooner.

Attached to the body in the pocket, soaked but legible, was a white correspondence card. It said:

A present for my mother.

──────────────── ★ ────────────────

Butler writes "richly textured police procedural(s)."

—Kirkus Reviews

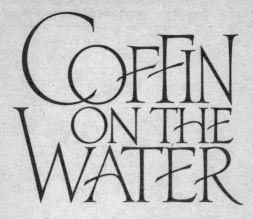

COFFIN ON THE WATER

Gwendoline Butler

WORLDWIDE.

TORONTO • NEW YORK • LONDON
AMSTERDAM • PARIS • SYDNEY • HAMBURG
STOCKHOLM • ATHENS • TOKYO • MILAN
MADRID • WARSAW • BUDAPEST • AUCKLAND

To J.K.M.

COFFIN ON THE WATER

A Worldwide Mystery/February 1992

First published by St. Martin's Press Incorporated.

ISBN 0-373-26090-3

CONTENTS

ACKNOWLEDGMENT

I would like to thank William Kelly of the Port of London Authority, Gravesend, for the kind and patient way he answered my questions about tidal waters of the Thames and what would happen to a body deposited in the river. He also told me the best place to drop one in.

I wish to thank my father, Alfred Williams, and my brother, Alan Lee Williams, both Freemen of the River, for their help with documents and diaries.

Any errors I have fallen into are entirely my own.

ONE

THE DELIVERY

IT WAS THE BIGGEST FEAST since the feeding of the five thousand, or so it was felt locally in Greenwich, and their outliers, the Hythe and the Wick. In the spring of 1946 the General Assembly of the United Nations was entertained to a banquet in the Painted Hall of the Royal Naval College. Premier Attlee welcomed them. The feast was austere, in tune with the rationed times: a soup, game, and a pudding, but the wines were good.

Present, in a purely professional capacity and not eating, were Chief Superintendent Dander, and Inspectors Warwick and Banbury. Also there were a troupe of young detectives-in-training, and among them John Coffin and Alex Rowley.

Also present was a murderer-to-be, like a bridegroom in waiting.

The bodies came later.

THE BODIES CAME DRIFTING in, delivered by the river, bearing a greeting card as if they were a birthday present. The river is a part of this story; the river supported the bodies, carrying them on the tide to their appointed destination. A body dropped on a rising tide in the river somewhere as yet unknown, between Deptford and Greenwich, to be carried up river, then back by the ebbing water towards Fidder's Reach where it will be deposited on the mud on schedule. Or so the killer thought.

Looked at later, as through the eyes of John Coffin, young detective still on probation, it was a hell of a journey they made for the hell of a purpose.

What a case to test the nerve. He was on the edge of things in that first big case and he knew it. Yet the fact that he was so, helped in the end. Indeed, led to its solution. If you can call a solution what was so terrible a resolution.

At that time he had a world to discover and a life: his own. Once in June 1944, he thought he had lost it, and once nearly had, but the shell from the Ruhr didn't quite do it. He came back from the dead, as we do occasionally. Now he had to find out what that life was worth and make something of it. The world was London, 1946. He joined the police.

Why the police? He wasn't widely known among his pals as an idealist or a law enforcer, but he must have had something there. One of his fellow police-cadets had wanted to be a ballet dancer. You could never tell where your feet will lead you. Give him ten years or so and he might know the answer. And when he did, would it be the diary of his years?

Around the first body the dark, oily water moved sluggishly, heavy with all the filth it bore. The body was not its only burden. Nor the first body, nor to be the last. Ships, tugs, barges had passed through it for decades, each generation depositing its own share of muck, coal dust and oil. Here at Greenwich the river was lined with docks and wharves so that the water lapped upon stone, not grass. Factories and warehouses shoved themselves up to the banks with their own unpromising war-strained profiles, nose to nose. Here and there a bomb-broken nose showed itself but the essential face of the docks and the river was unchanged, which might have surprised the bombers. Across one wall someone had written: 'Down with Adolf', making his mark on one warehouse. The rain was washing it away: Hitler's was a name from the past already, one you didn't bother with, and a wag had written underneath: 'Down with Stafford Cripps'.

It was visible from the railway which passed near at this point, adding its own dust to the dirt already delivered by the centuries of passing trade.

From the tops of trams and buses running down the main road between Greenwich and Woolwich on the one hand and Deptford on the other the river could not be seen, but you could always smell it.

The smell of the river might have been the last thing the victims had in their nostrils before the breath went out of them.

Looking down on the river from Greenwich Park was the small dome of the Royal Observatory. General Wolfe, victor over the French in Canada, stared down from his statue on the Royal Naval College housed in Wren's great buildings, once destined to be a palace. If you walked along its riverside façade you could fancy yourself in Venice.

The police station was away from the river, at the bottom of the hill not far from the Deptford Road, and was presently housed, due to the Blitz, in an old school. Nearby was a factory which exuded a pungent smell, at once oily yet sharp, not exactly pleasant but somehow homely. A smell you could recognize and live with. To the locals it was the concentrated essence of South London, that smell. Men in the army in Germany or in the Middle East had been heard to say: 'I wish I could smell Deller's again. One whiff and I'd know I was home.'

The smell was exceedingly strong in the police station, so strong that after a while you ceased to notice it, although it always hit you first thing in the morning when you experienced it with a crystalline sharpness.

It was a soft summer's day, the light luminous and golden, a haze over the city making every view gentle and romantic.

And the first body was already on the way.

Do you like bodies? Dead bodies? Naturally you do not. But in Greenwich, 1946, there was a man who did and he was waiting for this one; whenever life landed one near him he thought of it as a bonus. His actual contact with bodies was minimal although not negligible.

When the murderer first saw Rachel Esthart it was before his interest in dead bodies had become so particular and intense. He had gone looking for her, no other way of putting it, because he wanted to see what she was like. When he set eyes on her he was both fascinated and repelled. A *monstre sacré*, he thought, quoting. *Vénus toute entière a sa proie attachée.* He himself was much more than a bystander, by nature, more of a precipitant.

In the police station Sergeant Tew, born not in this district but further down the river at Rotherhithe, and only just come into Greenwich on his promotion, was very conscious of the smell of Deller's as his breakfast digested: scrambled, reconstituted dried eggs which his wife had managed to make extraordinarily indigestible.

He was standing at the wooden counter which protected him from the public, writing some notes in his careful, legible script, remembering at one and the same time the public events that would demand the attention of them all soon and a private message from his wife to call on the fishmonger on his way home for some whale steak. He hated whale steak.

A white hand fell upon his arm. It looked soft and feminine with delicate if grubby fingers but its grip had force.

He looked up. He was a tall, sedate man who was sometimes lucky, sometimes unlucky. It was what marked him. He could almost tell which it was the moment he woke up. Today he had felt unlucky.

'Officer, I need your help.'

He saw a tall, slender woman dressed in a plum-coloured velvet coat trimmed with dark fur. She wore a tiny saucer hat of copper-coloured feathers which no one in Greenwich would have recognized as the creation of Paulette of Paris circa 1929, but which the

Sergeant's innate sense of style told him was not the sort of hat his wife wore to church. Beneath the delicately pleated hem of her dress peeped a pair of pointed grey suede shoes. Everything she had on from hat to shoe needed a good brush.

'I request your assistance.' The voice was deep, commanding, with every syllable beautifully enunciated. 'In fact I demand it.'

She had immense black eyes.

He straightened himself from the paper, brought to order by the voice. All his life he had been brought to attention by such privileged voices.

'Madam,' he began. You didn't say Missis or Mother as you might have done to a less educated voice. 'What can I do?'

'I want you to help me find my son.' The hands were held together now, twisting, plaintive. Thus might Desdemona have held her hands out to Othello. Or Cordelia. They were pleading hands, eloquent hands, theatrical hands.

'Can I have your name, madam?'

She ignored this request.

'It's what the police do, isn't it?'

'Yes, ma'am. If we can. Now let's get this all clear. It's your son? Missing, is he? How long has he been gone?' He decided to leave names and addresses for the time being, he could sense this was a tricky one.

'Seventeen years.'

He didn't answer: all comment was knocked out of him. Seventeen years. He had been about thirteen himself. It was pre-war, and that was already history.

This was how he described it later: So, I said. That's a long time, madam, how old would he be? Twenty-two if he's still alive, she said. Then she said that she'd had a card saying he was sending her a present. But it hadn't come.

'A card?'

'Yes. A correspondence card postmarked Greenwich. Stamped, came through the post. It said: "A present will be delivered today from your son." That was two days ago. It hasn't come. So you see, he cannot be far away, I have to find him.'

'Perhaps the present will come along later, ma'am. And him with it.' He began to form a sentence in his mind about the Salvation Army finding people, when he remembered that this missing son had been gone seventeen years, since the age of five.

She was having a strange effect on him: he had the feeling that if he asked his limbs to move they would not answer his command.

'You've had a bad time,' he said awkwardly, surprising himself with his sympathy.

Three men appeared through the swing doors behind him: one older man in a dark suit with untidy hair, two young men, one very dark, one very fair, with golden to auburn hair.

They came on stage moving like veterans, natural actors, and dead on cue.

'So that's it about the Royal visit,' said the other man: Detective-Inspector Banbury. 'Now you know what's what. And you can stop thinking about the Shepherd business.'

He was only half joking: they had recently been dealing with the murder of a prostitute in a caravan off the Woolwich Road, an unpleasant murder. And there had been complications with a child. He had been surprised at the effect on his two young men and would be adding his judgement to his report on them. They had reacted too strongly. Then he looked across to where the woman and Harry Tew still confronted each other. She was keeping up a soft babble of sound. He walked across. 'Come on now, Mrs Esthart, sit down and we'll see what we can do.' Over his shoulder he said: 'Ring up Angel House and ask someone to come up here and fetch Mrs Esthart. Number in the desk-book.' He had written the number there himself. For good reason.

'She's had a drop, I think, Tom.' Tew was dialling. Presently he said, 'No answer.'

John Coffin came forward: 'I think I can help. I know who to get. A girl called Stella Pinero. She lodges with Mrs Esthart. It's all right, sir, I've got to know her quite well. I've met Mrs. Esthart once or twice. Alex and I both have. Good morning, Mrs Esthart. Stella will handle this.'

'Stella? This is John. Could you come down and collect Mrs Esthart? I think she needs help.' He hesitated. 'She's in some sort of trouble.'

'WHAT'S IT ALL ABOUT,' said Harry Tew. 'Who is that?'

'Rachel Esthart,' said Inspector Banbury. 'A famous lady and I'll tell you why: she's been under suspicion for murder for nearly twenty years.'

SEVENTEEN YEARS AGO, Rachel Esthart, an actress at the height of her power, famous, glamorous, wealthy, had suffered a terrible tragedy. Look at it how you will, calling her guilty or not, it was tragic.

Banbury said: 'Seventeen-odd years ago her son was drowned. She took him out for a picnic. Or so she says. But it turned out later she had left her husband after a quarrel over a love-affair. She was jealous. She'd been drinking, and she wasn't used to drink. Ran away, taking the boy. They were both missing. She turned up later, wandering around. Lost her memory, she said.'

'And the boy?'

'He wasn't with her. She said she didn't know where he was. Seemed surprised to be asked. But his body was found in the river. Drowned.'

'Nasty.'

'A lot of suspicion fell on her. But the coroner brought in a verdict of accidental drowning. Didn't stop the talk, though.'

'I bet.'

'And she would never accept that he was dead. Carried on as if he'd come back. Always said he'd be home again. And when he didn't, and didn't, she retired to Angel House and hid.'

'I remember hearing,' said Tew. 'It's coming back to me.' He thought Rachel Esthart looked calmer and more rational now, as if Banbury had had a good effect.

'Over the years she's often been in asking, roughly speaking, if we've got him. And of course, we never have. So what's new this time?'

In a wondering way Harry Tew said: 'She told me she'd had a card from her son saying he was sending her a present, only it hasn't come.'

He knew now what it was that was unlucky about the day: it was this visit of Rachel Esthart. It depressed him. Especially with whale steak for supper.

'She hasn't been in lately. To tell you the truth I thought she'd given up. Cruel of someone to start her up again like this as a joke.' Banbury felt angry.

If it was a joke.

THE DAY STELLA PINERO arrived in Greenwich was also the day a murder started to grow. Think of murder as a plant that has to have time to grow. Think of this murder as a plant with deep roots. The times get the murders that suit them. These murders were as bang in period as a page-boy hairstyle or a square-shouldered suit.

It is harsh to associate Stella with murder, pretty, charming, ambitious Stella, but the truth is Stella, and that little streak of ruthlessness in her, was integral to the plot. Yet, if it had not been her, one has to say, it might have been another girl. In which case the story would be different, and not the one laid out here. Yet even that may be doubtful. Probably it was all laid out, the way it would go, very early on.

Perhaps, as some philosophers suggest, there are alternative universes in which these murders are not taking place.

Stella Pinero, a young policeman called John Coffin, and another, Alex Rowley, arrived on Greenwich railway station on the same day. It was new boys' day. Stella Pinero going to the theatre, the two young men to their lodging-house and then on to report to the police station. Never mind it being Sunday. Actresses and policemen travel on Sunday.

One other person got off the train with them, but they were too busy noticing each other to notice him.

It was a cold day in March with a light rain just beginning to fall.

Stella walked up the platform by the side of a porter pushing a trolley with her bags on it; all she owned in the world was in those bags and she had to keep an eye on them. She was aware of the two young men following her, aware that they must be admiring her long, silken legs and hopeful that her stockings didn't have a ladder in them.

Without a word they hurried their pace so that they were just behind her when the porter deposited her bags. Her name was written in large white letters across the cases so they knew who she was from the beginning. Where she was going also. Theatre Royal, Greenwich, said a large label.

In the street outside an aged hansom cab with an elderly horse was drawn up, with the driver sitting slumped over the reins.

'I thought there'd be a taxi-cab,' Stella was saying in a puzzled voice.

'No taxis, miss. Not since the war. But there's old John and his horse.'

'Oh, the poor old horse. I don't think I could. I think I must be stronger than he is.'

But she had started to shift her bags when a tall, slender man came out of the station and cut across her path, apparently without noticing her, and jumped into the cab. He was driven off.

Stella stood there looking.

'Well, I'm damned. What a cheek.' John Coffin came forward; this was his chance.

Stella was staring after the cab. 'It's Edward Kelly. I saw his face. I don't suppose he even noticed me.'

Coffin knew the name. He liked the theatre himself. 'He's quite a plain chap, too.'

Stella said nothing. She knew all about Edward Kelly's plainness and what it did to you. Edward was supposed to exercise a kind of *droit de seigneur* over the junior members of the cast. Might not be true, of course, but she rather hoped it was.

Or did she? She was still a virgin. Well, more or less, she told herself. That is, rather less than more.

Alex picked up one bag, John Coffin the other, and together they walked with her to the theatre which could be seen from the station, lying riverwards.

Stella was friendly to them as they walked, chattering away telling them who she was and what a marvellous chance it was for her to work at the Theatre Royal, Greenwich, at this stage of her career. The Delaneys were real old pros; she was looking forward to working in their company. But Coffin got the clear impression that her thoughts were elsewhere.

Both young men were trained to notice things: John noticed that she was pale beneath her rouge: Alex Rowley noticed that she was stronger than she looked, she had picked up her case quite purposefully and it was exceedingly heavy. One of those frail toughs, he thought sardonically, half attracted, half put off.

The Theatre Royal, Greenwich, had been hit twice in the war, once in the first blitz and once by a buzz-bomb in 1944. Repairs had been kept to a minimum but it had a friendly old face, redolent of cheerful queues, with boxes of chocolates in the stalls and oranges in the pit.

Stella started to mime them a kiss, then changed her mind and delivered a kiss on each young man's cheek. It was a professional job, leaving no lipstick and hardly to be felt.

'Thanks, boys. Come around to my dressing-room one night and we'll have a drink. I don't know where I'll be living, the theatre is finding me a place. 'Bye for now.'

She disappeared into the theatre where they could hear her voice calling out her arrival.

'Well, that's her settled. What about us?'

For an answer John Coffin produced a piece of paper from his pocket. 'Mrs Lorimer, The Regency Hotel, Abigail Crescent. That's me and, I presume, you too. There's a map. Come on.'

Coffin said he knew a lot about the district, he had a connection.

'Mate of mine in the army, his dad runs a restaurant there. Vic Padovani.' Coffin remembered Vic well. A willing man but clumsy, an unlucky soldier. But likeable. 'We called him Robert Taylor.' With looks such as his, Vic could get any girl he wanted, and did, but they never stayed with him long. Unlucky. 'I'll look him up.'

They walked together up the hall towards Blackheath, not yet friends but ready to like each other, while recognizing they might have to be rivals.

They had met at Morley College, South London, which had been the venue for a special training course for the new intake for the Metropolitan Police, coming straight in from the army. Alex was the one who had wanted to be a dancer. Both John Coffin and Alex Rowley were members of a group specially selected for accelerated promotion. They had done their time on the beat in another part of London, taken the Morley College course, and were now detective-constables sent out, almost like rations, to this part of South Bank London by the river. They knew that there must be a personal file on them in the police archives with observations on their character, intelligence and behaviour. They were both conscious of having covered up something.

Mrs Lorimer's Private Hotel, over-grandly called The Regency, was part of a terrace of brick houses run up by a speculative building in 1850 and maintained in dubious repair by successive owners ever since.

Bombed in 1940, the hotel had not had a pane of glass in its windows for nearly five years, making do with yellow paper which let in some light but no views. Mrs Lorimer, a tall, grey-haired woman forever in a hurry, had been an air-raid warden and had not lost her air of command. She had personally doused fire-bombs in the great fire-raid of December 1940, remained calm when an unexploded land-mine descended on the roof of a crowded shelter, been awarded the George Medal, and been the scourge and terror of her neighbours.

She felt a certain stigma attached to having a police-constable (even if a detective) in the house. How would Lady Olivia feel? The old girl had a bottle of whisky at the moment and that was keeping her occupied for the time being, but when that was finished, she would be out and looking for battle. Mrs Lorimer sighed: she was difficult, but a 'name' and a family trust paid her bills.

She showed the young men to their rooms, almost with an air of apology, which prepared them for what they were getting: a low basement room for John and an attic for Alex.

Or they could choose. And could she have their ration books, please? Did policemen get extra, she had heard they did? She took their ration cards and departed triumphantly, muttering about individual butter dishes.

'Toss you for it.'

They tossed and John got the attic. He had been buried for twelve hours by a mortar shell on the way to the Rhine and was mildly claustrophobic as a result. Also, given a heightened perception of the world. Being blown up seemed to have peeled a skin off his eyes. He saw everything, fresh and clear as if it was a picture drawn by a sharp-eyed stranger.

His room had one tiny window which opened outwards with a jerk that would have robbed it of any panes of glass if it had had any.

From where he stood he could look down on the district in which he would be working. Below were the usual number of spivs, black marketeers, pimps, prostitutes, con men, thieves, and probably murderers. He would get to know most of them and if he did his job well they would disappear from the scene. For a while, anyway.

He could see right down the hill towards the river. The Royal Observatory was to his right amidst the trees of Greenwich Park. Down there but not visible was Wren's great palace, now a naval college, and a museum.

He found the view pleasing and touching. He noticed that the roof had an area with the tiles missing; when it rained his room would be damp.

Down there too was Stella and he meant to go on knowing her, but he wasn't thinking of her. Down there also was someone else he was interested in. A faceless, nameless someone at the moment. He had his own problem there. Coffin's own mystery, he thought.

There was the sound of music floating up from below. A window was open and in that room someone was playing a piano.

He closed his own window to go downstairs to call
on Alex. As he went down the stairs he could swear
that from behind one door he heard an old woman
singing. She was singing 'The Wearing of the Green'.
That would have been treason once, he thought, might
be even now for all he knew.

Alex was sitting on his bed polishing his shoes.

'Bed's hard.'

John Coffin sat down on the only chair. So was his
bed hard. They wouldn't stay here for ever, it was
temporary while they looked around, but anywhere to
live was hard to come by at the moment.

'Hope she's all right.'

'Who?'

'The girl. Stella.'

'Oh, she'll fall on her feet,' said Coffin; he knew a
survivor when he saw one. He was one himself.

There was a photograph of a pretty woman with a
young boy on the table. It must be Alex's mother.

'You got a brother, Alex?'

'No.' He was the boy in the photograph, then.

'Sister?'

'A sister, yes. Half-sister. What about you?'

'No.' John Coffin considered. 'Not as far as I
know.' He added, 'Wonder if we'll get anything to
eat?'

STELLA DID NOT REGARD herself as having fallen on
her feet.

She had run happily into the warm, dark womb of
back-stage Theatre Royal shouting that she had ar-

rived, and straight into the arms of Joan and Albie Delaney who were standing briskly engaged in one of their arguments.

They broke off to welcome her warmly, and at once got down to the essentials. 'Want you on stage with book this afternoon.' Joan Delaney never wasted words or time. 'Two sharp,' and she turned back to her argument with Albie, which appeared to concern Eddie Kelly who was sitting smoking astride a wooden kitchen chair, apparently indifferent to what went on.

'Now, Eddie, about the bloody lighting in the last act.'

Joan and Albie worked as a team. Joan was said to be the practical one and Albie the artistic conscience, but Joan's vaunted practicality existed only for theatrical purposes and did not extend to everyday life, where the pair lived in chaos. This showed itself at once with Stella.

'What digs have you got me?'

'Ah.' Joan wrenched her head away from Eddie who was saying softly that it was his bloody face that the bloody lighting was turning bloody green and he bloody well wouldn't have it. 'I couldn't get you in anywhere, dear. I tried old Madam Lorimer but she'd let her last room to two young men. You can share with us till something turns up. Doss down with us, Albie and me, in our sitting-room.'

'That's very kind of you.' Any doubt in Stella's voice was justified. The couple's quarrels were famous and their cuisine notorious. Then she remem-

bered that she was an actress and they were her boss.
'Thank you,' she said with false enthusiasm.

'Poor girl.' Eddie got up. 'Haven't we met?'

'Yes. At the station. You took the cab.'

'I had it ordered, my dear. In my permanent pay.
More or less. My gammy leg.' He had lost a foot at
Dunkirk. 'But I'd have given you a lift.'

Stella turned to Joan and Albie. 'Can't I sleep in the
dressing-room. Just for a bit? While I look round.'

Eddie moved nearer towards her. 'The girl will per-
ish. All the dressing-rooms leak. Albie, assert your
authority.'

Albie asserted his authority, and in a characteristic
way. 'Eddie, dear boy, you do something. Why not try
Rachel Esthart's? You seem to have influence with her.
She must have more empty rooms than Buckingham
Palace.'

'Rachel Esthart?' Stella couldn't stop herself. 'Is she
still alive?'

'Say that and she *will* love you.'

'But she was a *marvellous* actress.'

'Still could be, still could be,' said Albie. 'If she
hadn't hidden herself from the world.'

Eddie moved towards the telephone, carefully not
limping. 'I'll try. But don't say I didn't warn you.
Don't let her make a slave of you.'

Joan said, in a whisper, 'He hates you to see him
limping. The funny thing is—he's all right on the
stage. Wouldn't know. That's actors for you.'

At the door Eddie made a dramatic gesture. 'Rachel Esthart and you—I hope I know what I'm doing.'

Afterwards Stella thought that Edward had known exactly what he was doing and he was doing it for Rachel Esthart.

Edward soon reappeared to say Mrs Esthart would receive her, she actually used those words, which was Stella's first intimation of the regal way Rachel had sometimes. 'But we'll have to walk. I've got no petrol for my motorbike. Joan will send the bags up in a barrow with one of the men later on.'

On the way up Maze Hill, threading past the church, seeing the Royal Observatory on their left, Eddie walked fast, even while limping.

'I'll show you round, if you like. Interesting district. Where were you working last?' The perennial question between actors, what really interested them.

'Windsor Rep,' said Stella. 'Before that, Dundee. Albie saw me at Windsor. Offered me this. I wanted to be in London.'

'Oh? Any reason?'

'No. Just nearer the big managements. Tennent's, and that lot. My agent said it was the right move.'

'Ah. *His* right. Post-war theatre's going to be different from pre-war. Lot of the old names will be on the way down now. There'll be a new wave. Old management giving up, new ones coming in, new money, new ideas.'

'I'm looking forward to it.' Stella intended to *be* the new wave. Now the war was over, she felt a whole new world was beckoning to her with promise.

'Meanwhile you can't do better than be with Joan and Albie. They know change is coming. Watch them. If they go up, they may take you with them.' Or they might go down; that too was possible.

'I hope so.' Stella was getting breathless, keeping up with his fast, limping walk.

'They've got something good coming up. Marvellous publicity. A Masque for the Royal Family when they come to Greenwich later on. That's why they've got you. You'll be The Virgin.'

'Good Lord.'

'Don't worry. Nothing personal.' He laughed. 'But your predecessor as junior female lead—' Joan always played the leading lady roles herself—'didn't look too maidenly.'

'Do I?'

He gave her a crooked smile but did not answer. 'About Rachel Esthart, I'd better prepare you. The reason she's doing this Miss Havisham act—which you'll see for yourself when you get to Angel House— is she had a tragedy in her life. Lost her son.'

'Dead?'

'He was drowned. Rather mysterious. You're too young to remember, I expect. But she has never accepted he was dead. And who knows? She might be right. Perhaps he isn't dead. People do come back.' Stella nodded. The war had opened minds to strangeness and wildness in the world. Nothing was quite as ordinary as it had been before 1939. Anything could happen now. She believed him. It was the way things could go. Nothing was too fantastic to be ruled out now. It was part of how the world was, not solid, but transient, movable. Edward went on, 'she isn't mad. Or self-deceiving. Nor so much of a recluse as she pretends. She sees me; old friends like the Delaneys; it's the big world outside she's frightened of. It chewed her up once and she can't take any more. I suppose you could call it a depressive illness if you wanted. But she's a great woman, Stella, never forget that.' He stopped talking suddenly. 'Here we are. This is Angel House. Don't let her know I've told you anything. Let it be as if you didn't know.'

Angel House was a handsome brick building, probably built at the end of the eighteenth century, with a plain, dignified face. During the Blitz the roof had been damaged but the house had suffered no real hurt. Yet, without there being anything wrong with it, the house looked closed, turned in on itself.

Over the front door was the figure of a kneeling angel, an unexpected and baroque touch, but which provided the name. He rang the bell. 'I won't wait. Just see you in, then go. You'll be let in by Florrie. She was Rachel's dresser in the old days. She's no angel but you'll just have to make the best of her and get on with her.'

The door was opened by a small, plump woman wearing a dark apron. Sharp brown eyes were set in a sallow face.

'You've been quick,' she said unpromisingly. It was at this point (the very moment at which the two young men at Mrs Lorimer's were talking of her) that Stella felt her spirits dip. This wasn't going to be easy; she was used to life not being easy, you did not join the theatre expecting a soft ride, but unwelcoming digs she did hate. 'Madam said you'd be coming and where to put you.'

Inside, Angel House had a certain grandeur with a black and white flagged hall dominated by a curving staircase which rose splendidly, like a prayer, to a balcony above. But it smelt damp, and it was undeniably dusty.

'Come on, Miss Pinero.' She had the name off pat, a quick study, obviously. 'I'll show you where Madam wants you to go.' She led the way down the hall with a determined, shrewd little manner that confirmed Stella's belief that, as with so many dressers, she was an ex-actress. She threw open a door. 'It's where Madam used to sleep when the raids were on.'

The room was square with two small oval windows, decorated in the 'thirties style with heavy leather chairs and a big wooden desk, a kind of library, only instead of books the walls were lined with playbills, theatre programmes and photographs. A divan bed was pushed into a corner. Across it were thrown some sheets and blankets.

'We're a bit low on bed linen. You'll have to make do. We lost a lot when the local laundry got a doodle.'

'Thank you.' The sheets were fine linen, apricot-coloured, hemstitched and embroidered. The blankets matched. To Stella, the child of war and shortage, they were luxury.

She looked at the photographs. Rachel Esthart in part after part. What she was seeing was a museum to Rachel Esthart.

'She was lovely,' Stella said. 'Beautiful.'

Florrie's face seemed to fill out, put on another layer of flesh. So that is what she looks like when she's pleased, thought Stella.

'Thank you,' said a voice from the door, a true actress's voice getting across every wave of feeling, and what it said to Stella was: I appreciate your compliment but I do not need it. I am above and beyond anything you can give me.

Stella spun round.

Rachel Esthart was as tall as she was and just as slender. Her hair was dressed in soft waves, falling on her cheek in a manner fashionable in the early 1930s. She was wearing a long silk marocain dress of dark blue with a spotted bow. A long jade cigarette-holder rested in her left hand.

She was beautifully made-up, beautifully groomed. About her hung a strong scent of Chanel No. 5. Where did she get it, wondered Stella, to whom French scent was an unobtainable luxury.

Later, she was to learn that the scent and grooming represented a good day, the best, and that there were days when all this elegance became dusty and neglected, and the scent of Chanel was replaced by a sour, sad smell.

She came to know the smell of the bad days. But this was a good day, and it was why she had got in to the house. On a bad no doors would have opened for her.

As she looked at Rachel Esthart she had the sensation of a great many doors opening for her, a vista through which she looked towards success, money and fame. At once she felt tremendously excited. Ambition stirred in her like a live animal. She had always known she was an ambitious actress; now suddenly she saw what she could be. She could learn so much from this woman.

'Thank you for having me here.'

Rachel Esthart laughed. 'Well, you'll pay.'

'Oh yes . . . You must tell me how much.'

'I didn't mean in money.'

'Two pounds a week and your ration book,' said Florrie swiftly.

Don't be a slave, Edward had said.

'I knew you at once. You're Estella Beaumont's daughter, aren't you? Couldn't be anyone else. She died.'

'Yes.'

'What about your father? A lovely man.'

'Dead, too.'

'Your mother had marvellous technique but not much heart.'

'No.' There seemed nothing else to say. Besides, it was true.

'Your father was the other way. All emotion but not much technique. Which are you?'

'I'm nothing much at all at the moment,' Stella admitted. 'More my father's way, I think.'

'I can do better than that for you. If you'll learn.'

Stella had a moment of enlightenment. 'You looked me up.'

'Yes. In *Stage*. I always do when the Delaneys get someone new. You got the Ellen Terry medal.' Stella nodded. It was her first intimation that although Rachel Esthart might be walled up inside Angel House she minded passionately about the theatre still. 'But it wasn't until you walked in the door I knew you were your father's daughter.'

'I'll learn,' said Stella. My God, she thought. What an offer.

'I loved your father, you know.' Well, she was supposed to have loved many men. 'And I owe him something.'

'I must pay.'

'I'll leave all the financial side to Florrie.'

'Two pounds a week and your ration book,' said Florrie at once.

From the door, in her glimmer of pearls and aura of Chanel, Rachel said, her face full of mischief, 'You'll eat well here sporadically. Florrie knows all the best black-marketeers. She's related to most of them—and there's always the Italian restaurant on the Heath when you're short here. Florrie's cousin owns that, too.' There was malice and amusement in her voice.

She was gone, leaving Stella alone with Florrie.

End of Act One, she thought, curtain. Suspense building up.

'YOU'LL EAT WELL HERE,' said Mrs Lorimer, serving the young men with Yorkshire pudding and roast beef. 'I'm on very good terms with my butcher.' And with the local police, and with the Padovanis of the nearby restaurant. During the war she had insinuated herself into a position of power which she had no intention of relinquishing now peace had come.

'We passed a theatre on the walk here,' said John Coffin.

'Oh, you walked did you? There is an odd cab but you have to book it. I'm a keen theatre-goer. I get my complimentary tickets, you know, and if I can't go I send a friend. I was asked to give a room to a young lady actress, but it couldn't be done, the rooms were spoken for you.'

'Who is it plays the piano?'

'That's Chris Mackenzie: he works in the theatre on the stage management side. An old theatrical family.'

'And who is it who sings?'

'Singing, is it?' A shade passed over Mrs Lorimer's face. 'That'll be old Lady Olivia. Have some more potatoes. I grow my own at the back so they can't ration me there.'

Nothing more was to be said about Lady Olivia, John Coffin gathered. He wondered what her ladyship had done besides sing drunken, seditious songs. Probably been a terror with her blackout curtains.

His landlady interrupted his reflections. 'There's a message from your boss to say he wants to see you two this afternoon. You'll need to go on the bus. 54s do you.'

The two young men looked at each other.

'He's a marvellous man. I used to fire-watch with him. We all took our turn. His wife was killed in that rocket at Woolworths in New Cross. Doing the Christmas shopping, she was. A tragedy, but we've all suffered.'

Her eyes fell upon John Coffin who had been blown up by a mortar shell and upon Alex Rowley who had a badly injured hand when a sniper's bullet smashed across his fingers.

The two young men caught their bus, while Stella walked down the hill to the theatre. It was a Sunday, but a working day for them all.

SOME WEEKS LATER they had had, all of them, a rough time.

John Coffin and Alex Rowley had discovered that Inspector Tom Banbury, perhaps in reaction to the death of his wife, was not an easy boss.

The current crop of post-war crime in Greenwich, Greenwich Wick and Greenwich Hythe was interesting and varied. Nothing major, but most of it time-consuming and exacting. Tom Banbury did not spare himself nor his juniors.

A boffin from Cambridge had committed suicide by taking an overdose of barbiturate drugs, then lying down under a tree in Greenwich Park as night came on. A park-keeper found him. He had left no suicide note; nor was there any easy answer as to why he had done it. No money worries, nor domestic crisis. His widow said she could not understand it. He had been working during the war near Bletchley but was looking forward to a return to private life. Then a man came down from the Foreign Office and a blanket of silence descended.

A lorry parked outside the Sunshine Café on the Greenwich High Road burst into flames and was burnt out. Investigation revealed that it had been totally empty at the time, its load of food and tins having been unloaded sometime earlier. The lorry-driver and his mate, both of a low IQ, were arrested. They had the money for the sale of the rationed food still on them. The black marketeer was not located. A watch on the Sunshine Café and also on The Padovani Italian restaurant (the same owners) failed to produce results. But the sessions at the Padovanis' were highly pleasurable.

A woman, a known prostitute, was found shot dead in the caravan she inhabited on a bit of flat land down in Greenwich Hythe. She had been shot about six times, her body torn apart by large calibre bullets. Her death was linked with those of two people whose bodies were discovered a week later in their basement flat in Evelyn Street, Deptford; they had died together, probably about the same time as Connie Shepherd. Their son, recently demobbed, was missing. After a search he was found camping out in Epping Forest, where his only explanation seemed to be that it was his mother's fault. Connie Shepherd's error appeared to be that she was 'too soft'. The ex-soldier had with him a German gun he had picked up in Cologne. Connie Shepherd's young daughter who had lived with her was missing, and remained missing. The soldier claimed to know nothing about her, and so far no evidence one way or another had been found. It was a nasty case.

Both young men felt and displayed anger in this case as they worked, which was noted by Inspector Banbury. He too felt anger at the disappearance of the child but did not show emotion. The kid was dead, he knew it, everyone knew, but until they found her body, or what was left of it, there was no way forward. Inside, he wanted revenge for her, though.

Across the room on this warm spring day he could hear John Coffin taking a telephone call. 'Lower Thames Street. That's down by the docks. Right.' He had flushed red, then the colour drained away.

There was a strange atmosphere in this police station, somewhat alien to police work and perhaps due to those long-ago scholars, generation upon generation of them. The school had started its life way back in the 1880s as a London School Board Elementary School: Boys on the top, Girls in the middle, and Mixed Infants on the ground. Then in the 1930s the London County Council had raised its status, turning it into a Grammar School. Status but not appearance. The architect employed by the old London authorities had a strong house style, a kind of modified Venetian Gothic, so that one red-brick London school closely resembled another. Banbury had gone to such a one himself. So had Connie Shepherd, so had her child. It made a link.

Coffin came straight across. 'A workman digging on a site in Lower Thames Street found a foot wrapped in newspaper.'

The two men looked at each other. Alex had gone white.

Coffin said, 'The foreman said a child's foot.'

'Get across. Both of you. I'll follow.'

There was no denying that Alex Rowley had a way of showing awkward emotion. Banbury felt he needed a safety-valve. Marriage might provide it. He seemed the sort that might marry young.

He had seen them both with Stella Pinero in the Padovanis' restaurant. Separately. Not together.

The foot found on the waste ground of Lower Thames Street was that of a child. It was probably that of Sybil Shepherd, but there was no proof. The foot had been severed at the ankle. The search continued. Nothing more was found on that site.

Shortages of all kinds impeded quick work. Severely rationed petrol meant that most leg-work was literally done on the feet. Lack of telephone lines cut into police communications, creating delays and frustrations.

Space was one of the shortages at Greenwich Wick police station. Privacy was at a premium. From where he worked in his own crowded corner, John Coffin could see both his boss, Tom Banbury and Alex. Likewise they could see him.

But at least he had a window. From his window he could see German POWs clearing the ground where a colony of new houses was going to be planted. There could be a bit of Sybil Shepherd there. Who knew?

He walked over it every day on his way to eat lunch at the Trafalgar Arms public house. He always looked now for evidence of unusual disturbance. Observation counted for so much in detective work. He was exploiting his sharpness of vision.

But it hadn't helped so far with the Shepherd child. This search looked like their biggest problem, a harrowing and horrible one. He didn't see it as more than that then.

He walked across the cleared ground on the way home.

His mind was burdened like a pack-horse with bundles of problems picked up in the day, a tightly packed box of private concerns carried with him all the time, and the odd perplexity that was a weight for a while, then put down and of no importance.

Today he was asking himself if the foot was that of the missing child or, as some thought, a left-over from the Blitz which had defied decay? The newspaper ought to give some help there. Then, if the foot did not belong to the Shepherd child, ought they not to be searching for the girl as alive? Could he trust his boss's judgement on this? Could he trust his boss?

As he walked, his mind performed the throwing away act that lightened his burden every night. First out went the worry of his boss: probably nothing there; next went Alex: let that lad get on with his own troubles. Professional problems did not go away, but were deposited more comfortably about his person so he could think about himself.

He thought: Although I don't like living at Mrs Lorimer's and shall get out of it as soon as I can, we are an interesting lot. There's Lady Olivia for one. Then there's Chris Mackenzie always composing on the piano, and when he's not doing that he spends his spare time carving model toys—aeroplanes and motor-cars. These he sells. Gets a good price, he says. Sociable chap. Gave us a drink on our first night here from some Padovani wine, and didn't complain when a glass got spilt. Said he always spilt a glass himself on principle.

Mrs Lorimer complained, though, next day and said Alex had spilt some as well. He denied it, but I know he had because it was all over the Penguin I'd lent him.

He walked on.

He had plenty to think about. When he got home that night, just over one month since he had arrived in Greenwich, he began to write an *aide-mémoire*. A misnomer to call it a diary.

He dated it carefully: April 29, 1946.

And then at once burst into a flow of words about his own personal and private problem.

What Aunt Gert told me: that in August 1922, she thinks the third day of the month, a child was born to Julia Fairbain who later became Julia Coffin, my mother. This child was put out to adoption within the next two months. And Gert

said she did not know the sex of the child, nor
who adopted it. Her sister told her nothing about
it, except that the event had taken place. In 1943
just before she died she told Gertie that the child
was still alive and had been in touch with her. She
wanted the two of us to get to know each other.

Aunt Gert kept quiet about all this because she
didn't see what I could do. Also, I was in Germany, then in hospital. When she heard I was
going to be a detective, she thought I ought to
know.

He raised his head from his notebook; he had chosen a red one as being strong and positive. These
qualities might rub off on him. Then he wrote:

Aunty is still alive and bearing down on me to
come up with an answer.

Query? Aunt Gert is becoming senile. Did she
invent the whole story?

If she did not invent it, then can I rely on the
details?

If she is passing on those details accurately,
then did my mother tell the truth?

He raised his head again. One thing was sure: she
had not told much of a story.

Pinned in the back of the red notebook were the
only pieces of documentation that his aunt and mother
had produced.

A picture-card, addressed to his mother, postmarked, Charlton S.E. and dated October 1940. It said:

Got home safely, so don't worry. The Blitz won't get me. I'll keep in touch.

The picture on the card was of a church and a road.
There was also a single sheet of newspaper. The *Kentish Mercury* for November 1941. It carried various stories. Also a column of births, deaths and marriages.

That was all he had, and all he would ever have to help him find his unidentified sibling. If he had one.

I have been to the *Kentish Mercury* [he noted in his *aide mémoire*], and read the whole of that week's papers through. I got no help.

I have walked around Charlton and I cannot identify the church or the road.

Think of it as your little hobby, he told himself, when you're not looking for the murderers of prostitutes, and missing children. Or falling in love with girls like Stella Pinero.

STELLA WAS NOT WRITING an *aide-mémoire*, but she had one great friend to whom she was writing a letter.

Thanks for your letter. Funny to think of you in Stratford. You seem to be getting some marvellous parts. Lucky of you to get your teeth into Ophelia. No one's offered me Ophelia here, but I'm not doing so badly. What do you say to *Major Barbara, Trelawney of the Wells,* and Amanda in *Private Lives*? And I stand a good chance of being Prince Charming in the pantomime at Christmas, so beat that. Also, there's something more in the offing but that's still a secret and I mustn't say.

The Delaneys are super, marvellous management. They've got some tremendously good people here. No one I've worked with before but *names*. Edward Kelly, for one. I mean, he really can act. I'm learning a lot.

There's another bonus too. Where I live. Angel House belongs to Rachel Esthart. Yes. That surprises you, I bet? Remember how we used to try to be like her. Now I don't have to try. I feel as though I practically *am* her, I see so much of her, and she's teaching me. Proper lessons. We go through my parts. She's got a room rigged up for a theatre. I haven't told the Delaneys, but I think they know.

Here the writer showed a hint of nervousness. Rachel Esthart had so powerful a personality. I must struggle to be *myself* as well as her, she thought before going on:

There's a funny thing about her. She never goes out. Well, hardly ever. I have heard tales that she sometimes hires a car and drives to a first night where she sits in the back of the box wearing white gloves and clapping. Or not clapping if she's displeased. Then she has supper at the Savoy and drives back.

So she's not quite a recluse. The house was a shock at first, but the bit we live in is all right. The rest, cobwebs, dear, and dust. Apparently the Miss Havisham thing goes back to when she lost her son. It's a form of agoraphobia, I suppose. It's what Miss Havisham could have had, if you think about it.

But there's something even odder. She drinks a bit. And one night she let *out* that she doesn't believe her son *is* dead. Just gone. One day he might come back. And these last few days she's acted as if she'd had messages from Heaven that he's on the way. Oh, poor lady. Most of the time she's so sane, too. I suppose it's the gin talking. We all have our fantasies.

I won't tell you mine, but I *will* say there are some gorgeous men here. Two policemen (yes!) One so fair, one so dark. And there's Eddie Kelly. And a pretty good musician who's our stage manager.

I think I've clicked. It might even be the real thing. There's something very sexy about a slight maiming, isn't there? The Byron thing. He's very attractive, rather brutal, I suspect.

Stella finished her letter and posted it.
That afternoon she got the call from John Coffin

which obliged her to go to the police station and collect Rachel Esthart and take her back to Angel House on the bus. A journey not without difficulty as Rachel was withdrawn and hostile. The sympathetic union between them was now so strong that Stella felt sick, angry, and yet frightened at the same time and knew this was how Rachel felt.

Florrie met them at the door, and Stella handed her silent charge over.

'Come on, Mrs Esthart, love. What happened?' she said to Stella.

Stella told her side of the story.

'Come on, love,' said Florrie to her mistress. 'What's behind it? I knew something was up, keeping it to yourself, weren't you? Tell old Florrie.'

For answer Rachel produced a card. It was a plain white correspondence card with a gold deckled edge, a slight pink shadow, hardly a stain, marked one edge. It said:

I am sending a present to my mother. It will arrive on May 1st from my mother's son.

'Yesterday was May 1st,' said Rachel. 'It's late.'

She was like a child whose birthday had been overlooked, but at least she was talking.

Florrie said defensively, 'I blame the drugs they give her. She'll be herself when they wear off.'

'I am myself.'

'I think that card is wicked. A cruel joke.'

With the bleakness of returning sanity, Rachel said: 'Either the card is honest, and my son is around. Or somebody hates me.'

Next day the first body arrived, afloat in the river, but late for its appointment. It had got caught in the chains attached to a string of barges. This had delayed its transit up river. Otherwise the tide would have deposited it sooner.

Attached to the body in a pocket, soaked but legible, was a white correspondence card. It said:

A present for my mother.

TWO

THE SHAPE OF THE MURDERER

THE FIRST BODY, that of a young woman, was found soon after dawn by a lighterman going to work his barges. The tidal river has its own pattern and sets its own working hours, so he was early to work. The tide rose about five o'clock, but it was full summer and a fine day so he had light enough to see what was there at the wharf on Fidder's Reach.

When he had taken it in, Will Summers, lighterman and waterman of the river for thirty-odd years, not without experience of dead bodies, was sorry that he had seen so clearly. I'm never going to forget that sight, he told himself, I shall never forget that girl, poor kid. She's going to come back every so often and be like a member of the family.

He knew it was a girl from the clothes, otherwise he might have been confused, for the face had been terribly beaten by the chains in which she had become entangled, and a piece of rope had lashed her legs, tearing at them. There were no fish much in the river, but there were eels and some of them must have found her. Or perhaps a river rat, venturing out at night to eat. The pathologists would identify the likely causes of the marks.

She was wearing a pretty flowered cotton dress. Or at least, it had been pretty once, brightly coloured in red and blue, but it was stained and dirty now. Her shoes had gone, but a necklace of white beads remained around her throat. Will Summers took that fact in because of all the things about her only the white, china beads remained unspoilt. They gleamed in the water. They were what he had first seen and reached out a hand to touch.

The water moved darkly around the body, unpleasantly thick and brown. The barges had been towed along late yesterday and lined up in a string to be unloaded on Ellers Wharf. At some point they had found the body (or it had found them) and brought it along with them.

'I never saw that happen before,' said Will Summers to himself. 'First time I ever saw that. But anything's possible in the river.' The river was a living entity to him, a character fully alive and operational in his working life. He respected it and feared it. Never more so than now. Then he saw how it happened with the girl. It was her hair, her lovely long and beautiful fair hair, that had become entangled in the chains. She would have to be cut free.

He made for the telephone to call the police. On the wharf was a wooden shed which served as an office, the telephone was in there. His foreman was sitting down going through some papers and drinking a mug of tea. He looked up in query.

'I've got a deader.' He dialled 999. 'And I don't like it, Ted, I don't like it.'

'They're none of them good.'

'You haven't seen this one...' His hand was trembling so much that the telephone shook. 'I can't get this bloody number.'

Ted took the telephone from him. 'Here, let me.' He put his mouth to the instrument and shouted. 'Police.'

After he had got his message across he went outside to take a look for himself. Soon he came back and went across to a cupboard on the wall which he unlocked, taking out a bottle of colourless liquid to pour good helpings into two mugs. 'Here's yours, Will. Drink up.' It was rum, transparent before the burnt sugar was put in to colour it, and immensely strong. Never ask where it came from. 'It's my silver wedding anniversary today. Nice way to bring it in... Not that it's not better in some respects than the day itself. I was out of a job and on casuals. No way to start a married life. At least this war's put us to rights there, Will. Never be out of a job now.'

'No.' Will drank up. Both men had seen the river in the Depression when men crowded at the dock gates to be picked out one by one for casual work, favoured men first. The war, in a way, had been a godsend. 'Not in the docks, any road.'

'Not anywhere. It's different now. Got a welfare state now, you know. This lot know what they're doing.'

'They better.' He took a deep drink. 'You always were an optimist.'

The two men finished their drinks. 'So what about the one outside?' asked Ted.

'Murder. She's been murdered, that one.'

The news about the body was spread about the area with speed, reaching several centres where gossip was received and disseminated almost before the police knew themselves what had turned up there on the riverside. They were slow to react at first, thinking it just another suicide. There had been two already that year. The ending of the war had not brought peace to everyone. The last floater had been a young girl who had gone in with her lover, a coloured serviceman. He had survived, she had not. They were all the same, but all different, with the little eccentricities of dying that make each death unique. The hand grasping a piece of wood that it had clutched at as it went down, the body making its own bid for life, defying the mind; the body unclothed because death comes easier that way; the body in the top coat because the water is cold; they got them all. The murdered do not have so much choice, they are thrust willy-nilly into their departure with all the apparatus of their living about them. They cannot choose whether they die with their return train ticket to Waterloo in their pocket or a ham sandwich still stuck in their teeth. This too the police team had met recently. Connie Shepherd had been eating ham and the threads were still in her molars.

All those dead by drowning show the same set of post-mortem signs, this is where they are the same. But this is only true when the bodies are recovered from the water soon after death, for when putrefaction comes on then these signs are obliterated. Most bodies from the Thames were recovered soon. Such bodies most often displayed a froth of fine bubbles at the nostrils. If wiped away these bubbles reappear, pushed out from the sodden lungs.

The body newly arrived showed no such signs and Will Summers knew it as well as anyone. It was probably from him that the first stories came. He had an Irish mother and could tell a tale and usually did. Ginger McCaffey was a mate of his and distributed the news as well as the milk. He was certainly the agent by which the Delaneys and Stella Pinero and the rest heard the news at the Theatre Royal. Joan told the cast as she handed round mugs of coffee. They were doing J. B. Priestley's *An Inspector Calls* and it seemed appropriate. Up at Angel House they were slower to hear the news because they were not on Ginger's round, but Florrie heard when she called on her cousins the Padovanis for her meat. They supplied her with meat, butter, bacon and all interesting information. In their business you got to know a lot, and although taciturn Northern Italians, they were willing to talk to Florrie who was kin. Her mother had been English but they were willing to overlook that since Florrie was so totally in looks and spirit one of them. Only in her taste did she display her English mother; she rarely drank coffee but consumed quantities of sweet dark tea. The Padovanis called her their 'English cousin' and laughed at her when she was not there. But they respected her for living at Angel House, for her loyalty to Rachel Esthart, and for lending out money at interest, a good business woman.

They told her about the body and Florrie told Rachel Esthart. She considered suppressing the news but decided, after thought, that she'd better say. She had a presentiment that it would be wise. Or so she claimed afterwards.

The other great centre for the spread of news was the local library where Florrie went almost daily to change books for Rachel (she was at the moment reading Miss Heyer's *Faro's Child* and wondering if she should buy the film rights) and where the cast of the Theatre Royal went daily to read the newspapers which they could not afford to buy, so they said, and to steal the one copy of *Vogue*, which was rationed, if they could manage it. Someone usually could. At the end of the month they put it back, much battered, to the very great fury of the librarian. But in the library everything was told, and all items of news retailed like a good serial. As quite a lot of people changed their library books every day, including Will's wife and Ginger's mother, items of interest could be exchanged, added to and occasionally denied.

Through these channels the news about the dead body spread rapidly with comment added. Very soon the murderer knew what his audience thought of him. He began to see his face reflected in the public mirror. This greatly interested him.

The news was received by different people in different ways. The Padovanis had taken a frank and cheerful interest in the news, while at the library the elderly librarian had said girls should look after themselves better. She returned to her Elizabeth Goudge.

Rachel Esthart took the news calmly. She was in one of her downbeat moods after the excitement of the last few days. If she still believed her son was close at hand, she seemed to care much less. Perhaps she no longer believed he was alive.

She had, of course, been the victim of a filthy joke, and she had the card propped up on her desk to prove it, but she no longer seemed very interested, and if she was not, who else was left to mind?

Deep inside her own personal castle, Rachel Esthart heard about the dead girl with distant politeness. Florrie was relieved; her premonitions of trouble were wrong. She was very glad not to have precognition or telepathy or whatever. Her grandmother had been a witch; or so her mother (who had not liked her mother-in-law) had always alleged.

There was always the chance these powers had descended to her. In an Anglo-Saxon environment they would not be a comfortable attribute. But it would certainly show Ma Padovani.

So she told Rachel, who listened carefully. 'Poor girl,' she said sadly. 'I hate to hear of young creatures dying. There's been too much of that already in the war.'

Rachel had never closed her mind to the war, she had listened to all Churchill's broadcasts. The progress of the war in North Africa and Italy, and then in France and Germany had been followed closely on war maps. She identified herself with the army as if she was a young soldier.

'Florrie,' she said suddenly, 'I'm a bit scared. I feel death's getting too close. Will it be my turn next? Do you think I'm going to die.'

'No, love, no,' said Florrie reassuringly. 'When you are going to die, you don't know. It's unexpected.' She wasn't sure if this was true, but it was something to say.

'Do you think it's the war that produces a particular kind of murder—all those young men, seeing death, such violent and terrible deaths? No knowing what it might do to the mind. Not if they're normal. But who is normal? And could you ever be normal again if you'd been blown up? Or blown a man up with a grenade?' Her eyes wandered to the card promising her a present from her son. She still had it on her desk.

'You ought to throw that away.' Florrie was cross. 'It's rubbing.'

'Is there any gin left?'

'Right out.' Florrie was regretful on her own account. 'You finished it yesterday.'

Rachel sat for a moment in silence, then she said: 'I won't drink any more. That's it. Over.'

One brick in the wall she had built around herself was gone.

STELLA HEARD THE NEWS as she sat doing her face in her dressing-room. There was a brick out of her wall too, but in her case it was a real one. A bomb blast had

weakened an area of brick on the back wall of the
dressing-room, and one brick had become dislodged
so that a cold breeze played around her ankles. Someone had stuffed the hole full of newspaper but it did
not suffice to keep out the air of that chill summer.
She kicked at the paper with her foot; her hand deco-
rating an eye with mascara slipped and marred her
perfect cheek—the make-up there was just right, a
delicate apricot. She swore softly. At such times she
resembled a little cat.

She was considering what she had heard. Joan and
Albie had come straight out with the news and told
everyone. It might affect audiences; it might affect
everyone. One of the company had remarked that the
dead girl reminded him of '*l'inconnue de la Seine*'.

Stella had experienced a little shiver of alarm. She
had had a brush with violence herself recently and
knew how easily it could come about. It might even be
one's own fault. And now this poor girl.

Edward poked his head round the door. 'Hello,
poppet, a call for you. Albie wants you in the office.'

The war had cast a shadow over Stella's youth and
growing up. This separated her from someone like
Edward Kelly who had been adult in a world where the
lights had blazed all night with no blackout and no
bombs. His young world had had no rationing and no
clothes coupons. A leading lady in a smart West End
production expected to have her clothes ordered from
Molyneux and her hats from Reboux. It was a glitter-
ing stage which Stella had not known. On Edward
Kelly's nineteenth birthday, he had been appearing

with Noel Coward and Noel had sent him round a small bottle of champagne, then invited him back to Gerald Road. On Stella's nineteenth birthday she had been crouching in a cellar in the Theatre Royal, Bath, while German bombs fell around them, one of the so-called Baedeker raids.

Edward was a creature from a different world, hence the glamour he had for her, but she was really closer in age and spirit to the two young policemen and Chris Mackenzie, the stage manager and musician.

'What?' She got up hurriedly. 'Coming.' Joan and Albie had no glamour (this was not their style) but they were management and paid the wages.

She was on her way, dressing-gown flying. As she went past, he brushed a kiss on her cheek.

'I love you, poppet, know that?'

'Not you, Eddie.' The light turn-away was always best with Eddie.

He called after her. 'What's that face you were putting on? What face?'

'Candida,' she called back. 'For Candida.' It was to be her next big part, she just had the ingénue part in *An Inspector Calls*.

'Too hearty by half. Candida is pale,' he shouted— Edward was to play her clergyman husband. Albie, surprisingly, would be the poet: he could act thirty years younger than he was.

In the office, Joan and Albie were in consultation with Chris Mackenzie.

It was Chris who had said that the finding of the body reminded him of *'l'inconnue de la Seine'*, the famous nineteenth-century girl found floating and immortalized in sculpture. He said things like that quite often and they were never a joke. He was a disconcerting young man.

Now they wanted to discuss with her a technicality about Candida's entrance; there were difficulties.

Stella was cooperative. Anything they said. But all the time she was thinking of what Chris had said about the dead girl: it had sounded both calm and cruel. She did not like it that Chris could be like that.

She wondered what it would feel like living in Angel House with such news under her belt.

Well, at least, she knew some policemen. And the policemen knew her.

JOHN COFFIN and Alex Rowley went with Inspector Banbury to the scene of the discovery. The body had been removed from the water by then and placed on the riverside. For the moment it was covered with a blanket.

Inspector Banbury was in charge, the young men were present in a strictly subordinate capacity. They were there to assist and assist only, their sphere of action limited. In a way this was a help, or so John Coffin found. It freed the mind. He was able to look around and take it all in as a detached observer. Some of the things he saw he might not necessarily mention. Others he might review in his mind, then hand over to Tom Banbury. When the shell blew him up, then buried him, it took something away, an outer carapace, and gave him a clarity of vision. Life would replace the shell but meanwhile he saw all things new.

At the moment he was testing out Tom Banbury to find out how much of his individual vision he could hand over without seeming odd. Because the things he saw were sometimes ludicrously simple, yet might be important.

Such as the fact that although the girl had all her fingernails neatly trimmed, one nail and that of a little finger was long.

Then again, he saw that where the water had drained away from the body it had run into a pool that was half moon-shaped. That couldn't possibly be important or relevant, but it was certainly very striking. Stretched out like that, she reminded him of a picture seen in a history book of a sacrificial victim of the Aztecs with a shaped indentation at the feet where the blood drained, or libations were poured.

He looked up and thought that Alex had caught the reflection of his thoughts because he too looked up, shook his head and frowned. Coffin wondered if he would say something memorable or profound to round off the moment, but he didn't do so. All he said was:

'Cold down here. It's the wind off the river. Stinks a bit, too.'

There was a smell, sour and succulent, floating off the water now stirred by the sharp breeze. The same smell, with some addition of its own, came up from the dead body. He wondered if dead women smelt the same as dead men, there must be a sex difference, you'd think.

One thing was very clear as John Coffin looked down at the dead girl and that was that she had not died easily. In his life he had seen plenty of deaths, but they had mostly come very quickly so that it was over and done with before the mind took note. This girl looked as though she had had time to think about it and to know what was coming. Pain, too. Sharp, tearing pain and terror. A blow had fixed a mark down the side of her cheek and split her lip: she had felt that. There was another bruise on her chin. Her hands were swollen and water-sodden, washer-woman's hands, but they had scratches and it looked as though she might have fought back. Her neck was bruised. A strangling?

Her killer might be marked. He registered that fact.

But the main area of wounds was on the trunk. There were tears in the pretty summer dress where a knife had gone through, and large bloodstains about each hole. He could see five holes. He counted. There might be more elsewhere that he couldn't see. A white woolly cardigan, equally stained, had been buttoned across her dress.

Put on after the killing, he thought.

Banbury came across from the foreman's office like a controlled whirlwind, the gentle, concise way of speaking belying the activity he generated, and Coffin told him what he thought.

'Been buttoned back on afterwards.'

'Don't jump to conclusions. I've known the lab boys upset a few ideas of mine. Let them have a look and tell us what's what and then we start thinking.'

In the month in which he had worked with Tom Banbury he had learnt that his boss was good-tempered and hard-working, but very little else besides. He didn't even know what football team he supported or what beer he drank. If he had a secret life even that was a secret. It was a mistake to be so closed up, and for a policeman it was a downright disadvantage. You ought to appear to be open, even if you were not.

John Coffin assessed Tom's comment as being in line with what he already made of his chief. A good man but limited.

So he got on with his own thoughts in the way he wanted.

He could see where a stain was partly covered by the white jersey and had absorbed some blood from it. Put on afterwards, he decided. And not just for fun. Getting her into that, a dead weight, would not come easy. But he did it.

That was all they knew then. Later they were to discover the reason, but Banbury was never to say anything.

'There is something about the clothes that I will comment on,' said Tom Banbury. 'They look to me the clothes of a quiet, respectable girl. She wasn't one of Connie Shepherd's sort.'

The bare legs stretching before them had been pretty, sun-tanned legs, the feet well groomed with neat toenails. 'She wasn't flashy.'

'Wonder who she is?'

Tom Banbury shook his head and shrugged. 'There might be a name on her clothes. But I doubt it.'

Alex came back from where he had been talking to a uniformed constable. 'Surgeon's just arriving, sir.'

'Know who she is, Alex?' said Banbury. 'Any idea? Ever seen her before?'

'No. Unidentified.'

An unknown girl dragged out of the Thames: that would be the newspaper headlines. It would make the evening paper. There was a stringer from the *Star* there already, with a young woman from the *Kentish Mercury*.

'Somebody knows her.'

'Sure.'

'And we've got to find that somebody.' Banbury turned away to meet the police surgeon. 'That's how you do it, lad.' He nodded across to where the press stood, the first two had now been joined by another man. 'You can tell that lot there if they hang about there will be a description for them to print. They can help us get a name for her with any luck. As I said: somebody knows her, and somebody will be missing her.'

As John Coffin obeyed orders and walked across to the press, taking in that the girl from the *Mercury* had red hair and pretty ankles, he noticed an arrival.

A smart black car drew up to the kerb from which stepped, accompanied by what ought to have been a flourish of trumpets and felt as if it had been, a burly well-dressed man. The man gave him a quick, perceptive look and passed on, coat flying. Coffin had the same feeling he'd had when he'd encountered a General on the field of battle. It was a sparkling entrance.

Coffin knew his name but not his face. Chief Superintendent Dander, the Supremo of the CID in this South London police district, the nearest thing to God in Coffin's professional life, had arrived.

Coffin stood back and waited for his own boss to be walked over, obliterated. It didn't happen. Instead Dander quietened down, drew Tom Banbury aside for a long discussion in which Banbury took his full part.

The arrival of Dander aroused instant interest in the press, especially in the *Mercury* girl who said she'd met Dander before and where he went a story flowered, so what was this one here? There was a murmur of agreement from her colleagues. Coffin saw at once she had been put up as spokesman as being the one most likely to get an answer.

'You know as much as I do. Probably more, because you're allowed to use your imagination and I can't. You'll get a full description of the girl within the hour and then the more publicity you give it, the better my boss will be pleased.'

'He's having a nice chin-wag with Banbury,' said the local stringer from the *Star*. He knew everyone and all the gossip.

'It's breaking up now.'

Already the scene was crowded with figures, one in uniform, others in plain-clothes. One man was a forensic scientist, another the fingerprint expert. The ground was being searched painstakingly for clues. Later on, her body would get the same scrutiny for any evidence the murderer had left behind. Any contact leaves something, but it has to be found and evaluated.

The whole area was being corded off and a canvas tent placed over the body itself. Later, it would go off to the pathologist's table.

Where had once been relative quiet was now all action.

Tom Banbury and Charlie Dander were strolling on their way, still talking, still amiable. Dander must be more friendly than reports allowed.

'Wonder if I can get a word.' The *Star* man hurried forward. 'You know, he's quite bald under that Anthony Eden, that's why he wears a hat all the time.'

'He's a lovely man,' said the girl warmly. 'And I think it's madly attractive to look like that.'

'He told me once he lost all his hair from alopecia when he joined the Flying Squad before the war and had to tackle an armed villain single-handed.'

'I think he lost it when his first wife left him.'

'How many's he had, then?' asked Coffin.

'Two to day, isn't it, Win?'

The girl shrugged. 'No one's told me. Anyway, you can't wonder at it with policemen. Like being on the stage.'

'You mean policemen should only marry policemen?'

'Oh, witty. But that's about what they do, really, isn't it? That's the real alliance, the working one.'

Banbury and Dander parted with a brief handshake, Dander put on the speed, passed the journalists before they could get much out and departed with the same energy and flourish with which he had arrived. On the way he gave Coffin another stare and a quick grin. It was friendly.

I could work with that man, he thought. Also, how to make a good man a slave with one smile. Later he and Stella Pinero would decide that they were both the type that could be easily enslaved. Something to do with their body chemistry perhaps. Later still, he decided that it had all been worth it: a very valuable asset in the CID to have a Patron. Whatever it was, Alex Rowley, judging by the tight expression of his mouth when he looked at Dander, did not feel it. No easy response there.

Tom Banbury looked pleased with himself.

'There'll be something for you in a minute,' he said to the press. 'Meanwhile you can have a look round. No touching, though...' And to Alex and John Coffin: 'Come into the foreman's shed, lads. I want to talk.'

Will Summers and the foreman Ted had parted, presumably about their work, but there was a pot of tea and a trio of chipped cups still on the table. A tin of condensed milk offered sweetness and light. Tom

Banbury poured out the cups and sat down in the one chair. 'I'll be mother.'

Too happy by half, decided Coffin. I wonder what's up.

It was routine now, Tom Banbury told them. He detailed what their part would be, although they could more or less see what was coming, they had that much experience now. They were just little bits of the machine, pieces that must slot into position while at the same time showing intelligence and initiative. Was this always compatible? he asked himself. But questions were not invited. It might well be that his would be the last generation of young detectives to put up with this treatment. In fact, perhaps he would not put up with it. After all, he'd been through the war and that entitled you to a voice. But he wasn't going to say so this minute to Tom Banbury who was doing all the talking himself. Coffin got the impression that he was talking for the sake of talking, to relieve some pressure inside himself. It was a thing women did more than men, but a detective with a feminine streak inside him wasn't a bad idea. Perhaps all the best detectives had one. He might himself. Not Alex, though. From all he could gather Alex had been trained by his father to shoot himself if such a thought ever crossed his mind.

He heard himself being detailed off to interview Will Summers who had already told all he knew, but might be induced to repeat it with additions. You could never tell. Remember that Will Summers, although an honest man and truthful, was not an experienced observer of anything except the tides and might know more than he guessed. That was the idea anyway. So dig. Then he could do the same with Ted the foreman. He might be more difficult, having strong opinions and willing to voice them whether you wanted him to or not.

ALEX COULD DO the river police, with whom he had already been doing liaison work. Courtesy came into this and remember it. You had to tread carefully with all river men, they were a bristly lot. Binder was the man to see, Sergeant Binder. What he didn't know about the tides on the river and what they got up to was not worth knowing.

Alex nodded. He knew the rules. As a matter of fact, he liked the river police outfit and felt at home with them. A good bunch, freer, somehow, than the Met.

So they both knew where to go and they could go. Identification was the first priority. Here they should get some help from the clothes. These would be gone over inch by inch in the laboratory, but they would get a chance to see them. If they were lucky they would get a bit of help from the clothes, but it would lead to... they waited for the words.

More routine.

Tom Banbury drank some tea. From Coffin's own quick taste the tea was tepid and over-sweet, but the good cheer remained with Tom. Then he explained why. 'Dander has something for us. Not on this one.

The Shepherd child. He has a viewing of her that puts her still alive. He thinks we ought to check.'

Coffin understood the cheerfulness. They had all been brooding on the missing child, whereas the full horror of the present case had not yet quite come home to them.

'He's had information that a girl who sounds like the Shepherd child has been living rough in Lambeth. He's got a witness who claims to have seen her. Says the source is reliable. It could be. I shall check. I'll do that myself. I want to.'

They could both understand that. It would be one of the better moments of the job if it came off. The girl might not be in much of a state, probably wasn't, if she'd been living rough, but she'd be alive and they wouldn't be looking for bits of her.

'We'll meet later. When we get a view of the dead girl's clothes.' He put his cup down. 'Nasty stuff,' he said in a tone of surprise. 'Dead cold. Don't drink it.'

Coffin eventually ran both Will and Ted to ground a few yards down river where they were talking to a tally-clerk and watching stevedores unload some barges. There seemed a bit of a dispute about the details on the documents the tally-clerk was waving. A little high talking was going on, but they decided to end it when they caught sight of Coffin, and the matter ended amiably.

Will Summers watched him approach sardonically. 'Can't tell you any more than I already have. You policemen got time to waste, I reckon. Not so bad, eh?'

Ted shook his head silently. He did have something else to add but was wondering how to say it. He didn't like the police, never had, but there was nothing personal about it and he was prepared to give this young one a chance. He was glad it was him come to ask the questions. Apart from anything else (he was polite), he seemed better than most coppers. A nicer look to his face. It was his eyes. Their expression was not what you expected in a policeman, whose face usually said watch it. There was a hope, he thought, that the war might have brought them all round to one side. Anyway, we're the masters now, he told himself.

Will repeated his account of the morning: how he had come to work, seen the flash of something odd in the water, investigated and found what he had found. No more to it. He was surprised no one had noticed the body as the barges came trailing down the river, but she must have been masked.

Ted said the first he knew of it was when Will came and asked to use the phone. He had gone and had a look for himself but had nothing else to add.

'Not seen you before, have I?' he said.

'No.'

'Don't know the district, then?'

'Learning. My family came from round here. Before the war, though. I may have a bit of family here yet.' If he ever found it, of course, and Gertie had been telling the truth.

Ted nodded. 'It needs knowing.'

'I'll learn.'

'Better if you want to get on round here. Learn your
part too. Not what you might think. You're a worker,
remember. A member of the working class. Not a tool
of the government.'

'Never meant to be.'

'Ever read any Marx?'

'No.'

'Engels, then?'

'No.'

'You should.'

'Stow it, Ted,' said Will.

'Only explaining things to him. Making him think
a young man like him ought to think. He ought to
know where he stands. It'll be a help to him when he
goes around asking questions. Might help him to ask
some questions.'

'Thanks. See you sometime and have a talk about
it, may be?'

'Come and have a beer. The Black Horse is my local, you'll find your way there.'

'Any idea where the body might have gone into the
river?'

Ted shrugged. Will spoke weightily. 'She goes down
with the tide, she comes up with the tide. What goes
in on the ebb tide, it'll do a mile and a half and then
come back. If it was local, it could have been from the
Greenwich Pier. Known it used.' Will murmured
agreement. 'Be worth looking. It's very hard to say.
Try the river police.'

Coffin nodded. 'That'll be done.'

Ted turned back to the tally-clerk and resumed their discussion while Will Summers walked a few yards with Coffin. Whether out of politeness or to see him off Coffin wasn't sure. It felt like a mixture of both.

'He always like that?'

'Always been a bit left. Always disliked Churchill. Doesn't usually come out quite so strong. A quiet man as a rule.' Will had a soft, calm way of assessing things that reminded Coffin of Tom Banbury. Brothers beneath the skin. Probably went to school together. He must find out. One powerful schoolteacher could have imposed that way on both minds. 'You must have upset him. Or the girl.'

As he walked away Coffin was aware that he had been offered something but what it was he was not exactly sure. He would certainly get in touch with Ted again.

One of the journalists was still hanging around when he got to the road, waiting for snippets of information.

'Anything to say?'

'Nothing.' Coffin said regretfully; he would have helped if he could.

The man put his notebook away. 'Just as well in a way. We're so short of newsprint that half the things I write get edited out. But I hope.'

'Hope on.'

'Got a car?'

'No.'

'I'll walk with you to the bus, then... Your boss and Dander were pretty cheerful together. Raised each other's spirits.'

'Didn't really notice.'

'Of course they've got a problem in common.'

'What's that?'

'One of Dander's wives is Banbury's sister. Divorced now. But not forgotten. She sees to that. Drinks. Whether because she's unhappy or to drown her memories of life with Dander I couldn't say.'

'Thanks for telling me.'

'It's as well to know.'

Circles within circles in Greenwich, obviously, and those circles interlinked. Come to think of it, his own circle touched somewhere, if that sibling existed. But as the journalist said, it was as well to know.

HE WENT BACK TO WORK, carefully making out his report.

Since the police station was located in an old school the two young detectives worked in a room about three times the size that later generations would know.

Speaking for himself, and he had not discussed it with Alex, John Coffin was not grateful.

The office he shared with Alex was painted dark brown with large gothic-style windows; he had a big square desk and a hard wooden chair. Windsor style, the chair, he believed. Handsome in a kind of way, and certainly spacious. But because of where it was he felt as though he was still at school himself, you could smell the chalk, and the special kind of floor-cleaning oil that schools always used.

He disliked it greatly; he was never going to be at ease in this place, but he had to act as if he was. That was one rule he had learnt. It was a rule for the way up the ladder. He might break it, but he would certainly try.

Alex came in silently, and sat down at his desk to work. Everyone does it differently, thought Coffin. Him in his small corner and me in mine.

In the distance Tom Banbury's voice could be heard on the telephone.

'Any idea what's happening?'

'Not a lot.'

Events moved around them. They were supposed to make a picture. This didn't always happen; it didn't now. But don't say so, Coffin told himself.

'What about the river police? What did you get?'

'Not a lot. Chap said the body probably went in the river between Greenwich and Deptford Bridge. Would have gone with the tide, a mile and a half with the ebb, back with the flood.'

This was what the two lightermen had said, more or less.

'Got more details. Tell you later. But the chap pointed out that either the girl walked to the river with the murderer or was transported somehow. Only one or two places that could have been. Only one, Greenwich Pier, is open to the public. And you'd need something like a barrow to get a body along.'

John Coffin considered. A barrow did not seem likely. And what barrow? No doubt he would soon find himself looking for it.

Tom Banbury came in, he had his detective-sergeant with him, a man called Garston Frith. Not unnaturally Garston hated his name, so he was always called Geoff.

Banbury announced his position straight away.

'No good about the Shepherd child. Nothing at all. The wrong girl. Wrong height, wrong age. Right sex and that was about all.'

'No go, then? Was it just a lark?' A bold question from a young detective on probation like Coffin. He was chancing his luck in seeming to criticize Dander.

'Oh, Dander thought it was good information. It did seem genuine. Damn.'

So they were still looking for the Shepherd child and still hoping to find her alive. Every day that passed made it more doubtful.

'The body's down at the mortuary. Let's get down and look at the clothes.'

Events moved around them, they were supposed to make a picture as facts were thrown at them. Better not say too much aloud, though. Theirs was the shoe-leather job.

The police laboratory was the next to check in with a simple, first account of what she had been wearing. They would send a detailed survey later.

Simple clothes, pretty, inexpensive clothes. The under-clothes, knickers and a slip, were made of Celanese, an artificial silk, and had been bought at a well-known multiple store. No stockings. The shoes had gone.

The printed cotton had been home made. A lot of girls saved coupons by making over an old dress into a little floral skirt to wear with a little white blouse. Over the blouse she had worn a woollen cardigan.

John Coffin had noticed that the cardigan had been replaced after death.

It had been replaced to protect the envelope pinned to the pocket of the blouse.

Inside the envelope was a card. It said:

A PRESENT FOR MY MOTHER.

The message was set out in capitals cut from a newspaper. In which it was unlike the letter received by Rachel Esthart. The murderer had, perhaps, had some prudent thoughts.

Or perhaps he had thought about the water on the ink.

As it was, the card was sodden but legible. It was well stained, picking up various tints in the process. All the colours of the rainbow seemed to be there to Coffin's gaze, but a pallid, muddy rainbow, which had made itself up from green and blue drained from the coloured cotton to a reddish stain which reminded him of something. Coffin found himself staring at it with some thought.

The red stain on the card echoed the stain on the card sent to Rachel Esthart, and it prodded him to think something else also. A nonsense thought, probably. But there.

He was remembering a story heard in childhood. *Not* a story read by his mother as he went to bed: she hadn't been that sort of mother, more apt to read the *News of the World* than Hans Andersen. As a matter of fact, he'd learned to read from the *News of the World*, and still read it.

He was remembering the story of the child with the innocent eye and the Emperor's clothes. In this case his new sharp gaze seemed to see not a naked Emperor, but just a glimpse, as if the murderer were a fox, just a glimpse of the killer's tail. Not just the sight either, he got a whiff of the rank animal itself.

Then the experience faded, and all he was left with was a feeling as if something had gone back into hiding.

It had been a long, hard day, and when work was over so that he could return to Mrs Lorimer's, he was tired.

He had the notion that he had, that day, seen the shape of the Murderer. Not yet the face, still less the name, but an outline.

A man, strong, tall, with powerful hands, because the girl had been manhandled. A man who when he stood up against the window would block out the light. He looked like this himself: policemen did.

This sense of what he could see made him uneasy, restless. He wanted to shift.

At the end of that day Coffin had come to a conclusion.

He would not be staying at Mrs Lorimer's lodgings.

'I'll be moving out. Find something else. Better that way.' It would not be easy but as he trudged around South London he would be looking. Morally and imaginatively, anyway, he would be gone. Although he had the feeling one was not so easily shot of Mrs Lorimer's outfit. Staying there was probably an experience that stayed with you for life.

He stomped up the stairs to bed. Lady Olivia was not singing tonight, but Chris was banging away on the piano, something vaguely martial, a march perhaps.

He had one last look at the page of the *Kentish Mercury* for his private archives. He had a look most nights, nothing had emerged, but tonight, of all nights, he noticed a tiny row of ink dots underneath an advertisement. W. Clarke, the Butcher, Waller Road, S.E.8. He would think about that tomorrow.

Before going to sleep he looked out of his window. He could just see the roof of Angel House. He knew now that inside it was Stella, together with an eccentric woman to whom someone, who might not be her son, had sent a murderous present.

THAT EVENING Tom Banbury and Charlie Dander were having a drink in Charlie's local on Charlie's home ground. They met more often than anyone guessed. Not exactly friends, but people who needed to keep in touch.

They talked family business, but they also talked work.

Dander finished his drink. 'Better get home—about the message on the body: it may tie Rachel Esthart in some way with the murderer. But don't take that for granted. It's the romantic view. I saw your young men's faces: that's what they want. And it's because they're young. But what you've got to consider is that what you might have is a joker.'

He got up to go. 'I'll make a bet with you: you won't keep both your young men, keep one, lose one.'

He was off, making his usual splendid departure, leaving Tom Banbury in thought.

A joker, someone who had no real interest in Rachel Esthart, no love, no hate, no relationship, but who was using her as a joke, to give a bit of panache to his murder. Also to mislead. It was a thought.

THREE

THE STANCE OF THE MURDERER

COFFIN WAS SINGLE-MINDED. He sensed almost at once that Stella, going between Angel House and the theatre, and eating as she often did at The Padovani restaurant with the three young men in her life John Coffin himself, Alex Rowley and Chris Mackenzie, was really at the centre of everything, much more than she realized.

He stayed as close to her as he could so that he could be on this inner orbit himself. He was definitely on the perimeter with Tom Banbury, who saw he did the maximum leg-work and the least quiet cogitation at his desk. Not out of malice or anything of that sort, Banbury just liked keeping his thoughts to himself. And the young men out of his way.

He knew the outer side of what his boss Tom Banbury's investigation was because his activity was part of it. He knew that they were pushing out lines of inquiry on the clothes, physical details to establish the girl's identity. (She was only a girl: the pathologists put her as in the very early twenties.) He knew that Tom Banbury had interviewed all three women at Angel House. He had seen a transcript of all three interviews (Alex Rowley had been present, he had not) and

saw that the women knew nothing of the dead girl.
They were strangers. Nor did Rachel Esthart have
anything to say about the card which had come with
the girl.

The girl, her present, had been delivered. Rachel
Esthart flinched from that thought: she took her refuge, as once before, in hiding behind a wall of silence.

Who wants a son who sends his mother such a
present? Perhaps she did not any more.

And if not a son but an unknown enemy, is that any
happier a solution? Did Rachel Esthart deserve such
an enemy?

She would not say, admitted no idea of who it could
be. No answer was more or less what Tom Banbury
got, according to the written word, taken down by
Alex Rowley in his somewhat poor shorthand and
then typed out. It was on the record.

Stella the same, she knew nothing.

Florrie was even more terse, if that was possible.
The few sentences Tom Banbury had extracted from
her had been valueless, she was like all three wise
monkeys combined: she had seen nothing, heard
nothing, and could tell nothing.

So Coffin knew what Tom Banbury had got so far,
but did not know what he made of it.

In Coffin's book this was a black mark. Banbury
ought to talk to his young men. He was supposed to be
training them, wasn't he? It was a kind of apprentice-
ship.

Some details appeared, however, even in the bleak Banbury-Rowley transcript.

The letter had been a real letter, sent through the post, not delivered by hand. The post had been collected by Stella Pinero and handed to Florrie who took the letter in to Rachel Esthart.

The postmark was Greenwich, thought Florrie Padovani. Stella could not confirm this. She thought not: she thought you could not make it out. Rachel Esthart had not looked, but had taken out the card and used the envelope to light a cigarette.

When the news of the second card found on the dead girl was taken to Angel House by Tom Banbury himself, Rachel had gone into a shocked silence, something approaching a catatonic state, Coffin surmised. She could not speak.

Stella Pinero had attacked Tom Banbury for giving her friend the news so roughly.

Florrie Padovani, oddly enough, had had hysterics. Very Italian.

What Tom Banbury made of all this John Coffin did not know but what he could extrapolate was that the two linked incidents were 'genuine'.

In other words the three were truly surprised by the delivery of the first card, and appalled by the arrival of the second. They had no guilty foreknowledge; when Tom Banbury had asked Rachel Esthart why she believed her son to be still alive all she could reply, as far as she was able to talk at all, was that she had never accepted his death.

Tom Banbury's line was the orthodox police view: he had gone into the case, seen the case file, and knew that the coroner and police investigations had identified the drowned child of so many years age as her son. His own father had identified him.

The father was now dead; killed in one of the first bombing raids in London.

So the two views of Peter Esthart's death met head on.

'Impasses,' as Alex Rowley said. 'But intellectually interesting.' He was fond of making remarks like that. For instance, he said that he thought Tom Banbury was more preoccupied with the missing Shepherd child and did not want to devote time to the new murder.

A bloody baroque business, he called it.

But to John Coffin it was a human problem that had to be solved and he wanted to solve it. This was how he put it:

The dead body with the inscribed card, was one problem.

Rachel Esthart's son was another. So Coffin saw it.

Somewhere the lives of the two mysteries must meet.

Where, how and why, was what interested Coffin.

Somehow, it was not two problems but one.

To Tom Banbury it was a police matter.

To Coffin it was a practical and human problem and he wanted to know what it was all about.

That was when the duel between them opened. That was it, then, and not to be escaped.

Or so he thought. Because he was anxious, he discussed it over a pint with Alex Rowley in the Green

Man, which they had adopted as a refuge from Mrs
Lorimer's spartan hospitality. When you wanted an
easy half-pint now you went to the Green Man. When
you wanted something livelier, you went to the Padovani where you found the Theatre Royal company,
drinking coffee, learning their parts, or engaged in one
of those confidential discussions which made up their
life. Since meeting them Coffin had learnt how difficult it was to put on false eyelashes. How a girl felt
these days wearing a bustle (Indecent, dear) and the
best place to get an abortion. (But I haven't tried *personally*, love. The nuns educated *me*.)

A day and a half after seeing the body and its
clothes, it was the Green Man they went to.

To his surprise Alex started on the subject.

'What do you make of the Guv?'

'Banbury? Not a lot.'

'He's a good copper.'

'He's too housebound.'

'Deskbound, d'ye mean?' asked Alex.

'Housebound. He doesn't see out of the window.
No imagination. And he shuts us out. We ought to be
in there, right inside, know what he's thinking, working with him. And we aren't.'

Alex was silent. 'He didn't stay in the army long.
Came out. Don't know why. We're new, fresh blood.
I think he resents us.'

He did not seem to mind too much, but Coffin did.

He was very much aware of being on the edge, especially in this case. Excluded. He thought it was because Tom Banbury didn't like him.

Later, he learnt there was another reason. If he had
been a more experienced policeman he would have
taken a second look at that exclusion. And then a
third.

THE SOCIABLE HABITS of the theatre made it easy for
John Coffin to see Stella and the crowd at the Theatre Royal. He and Alex dropped in after work more or
less as they liked, either to see Stella play, or to gossip
with her in her dressing-room.

He got to know her friends and enemies in the
company. Impossible to be like Stella and not have
enemies. Her sparkle, that star quality which she had
been born with, aroused jealousy as well as admiration. The two went hand in hand. Moreover, Stella's
place at Angel House, with the patronage of Rachel
Esthart that went with it, made for envy.

But on the whole they were a generous, if emotional, company of players and if quarrels were
sparked off, then they were made up soon.

Coffin saw that alliances came and went at the
Theatre Royal, Nelson Street. Enemies today, friends
tomorrow, lovers possibly all the time. There was
usually a sexual bonfire burning somewhere at the
Theatre Royal.

It was the third day after the discovery of the dead
girl, who was still unnamed and with no known provenance except her connection with Angel House.

This fact was known, at the moment, only to a small
group of people, but would seep out in the end, probably through Florrie and her Padovani cousins.

Nameless and homeless, the girl had acquired a medical history.

She was a virgin; she had not been raped. There was no sign of an attempt at intercourse. Her age was probably in the early twenties. She was five feet and two inches, and in life weighed seven stone. A thin, small girl with blue eyes and brown hair.

Her injuries were striking: she had been manually strangled before immersion, for there was no water in her lungs. But after death she had been stabbed repeatedly and her genital area slashed.

The time of death was hard to establish, but she had probably been dead for three days. Or a bit more.

As HE LEGGED IT about South London, half grumbling, half happy, the other part of his mission came into place: he was relearning London's face, and with the learning rebuilding a little of his own life. Your life is a structure and it's up to you to put on the bricks. He had lived here as a child, forgotten it, now he was finding it again. Putting bricks back in a wall.

The river, the docks, the factories and warehouses that lined the wharves, these were his London again. With them he discovered London's countryside in the parks, scraps of common land and the bomb-sites, greening over as summer came on, blooming with wild plants bedding themselves down in town and domestic flowers flying wild.

The Theatre Royal in Nelson Street was an old theatre. Not old enough to have played to Queen Elizabeth the First or her Stuart successors, but old enough

to have welcomed their Hanoverian cousins. The
present building was Victorian, the time of its great-
est prosperity, when London stars had not disdained
to appear. Sir Henry Irving had appeared in *The Bells*,
and Ellen Terry had briefly graced the boards in
Twelfth Night. At the turn of the century it had become a music hall, and in the 1920s had lived under
the threat of being a cinema. But it had survived. Albie and Joan moved in and the theatre was saved for
drama. But the atmosphere of the old music hall still
hung about. Coffin always felt it when he went in. The
ghosts of Marie Lloyd and Albert Chevalier seemed to
be walking there still.

The stage door opened directly into a narrow dark
passage leading straight backstage. You could walk off
stage and be drinking a pint in the pub in Nelson Street
before the curtain had properly come down, and many
had. Marie Lloyd, for one.

Coffin loved this dark hole, it seemed the entrance
to a mysterious and vivid world. Symbols, left-overs
from the activity of this world, littered the passage. An
old pram that had been used by Window Twankey in
the last pantomime and was to play a part in *Candida*, stood against one wall. A sunbonnet hung on a
hook with a crinoline skirt suspended beneath it. A
fire-bucket left over from fire-bombed days now held
a wilting bunch of flowers, a forgotten present from
an overlooked admirer.

The stage door keeper, a wizened small man of liz-
ard-like appearance, greeted John. 'All gone, sir.
Curtain came down sharp tonight and off they went.

Something to celebrate.' He shook his head. 'Theatricals. Always celebrating. And half the time what they're celebrating doesn't come off. Actors are very melancholy people, you know, sir, when they haven't got something to celebrate.'

Coffin inserted himself inside the warm hole which was the stage door keeper's office. He offered a cigarette. 'Where did they go?'

'Up the hill to the Italian place.'

The walls of his office were lined with theatrical photographs from long past shows. Suddenly Coffin saw one that interested him. A young woman dressed in period costume together with an even younger man. 'That's Mrs Esthart, isn't it? And Edward Kelly with her?'

'Yes. Mad in love with her then, he was, you can see it in the photograph, but she never had any time for him. Just before her trouble hit her, poor lady.'

Rachel had written, in a large, dramatic hand: 'Love from your Nina' across the photograph.

She sent him love then, thought Coffin, and then she took it back. A man might mind that. It did not look like love in Eddie's face. Admiration, but love, no. Not direct, sexual love.

The Padovani was reminiscent of a Soho restaurant of the 1920s when Pa Padovani had arrived in London as a young waiter. He had reproduced his first workplace faithfully from the hand-written menu in the window to the draped red curtains. Inside, the tables were covered in coarse white cloths with spindly black chairs for the diners. On the air was always the

smell of grilled meat and cigars. God knows where the
smell came from these days. He probably had it bottled. The Padovanis had prospered, returning from a
short sojourn of internment to carry on their restaurant. Several Padovani daughters had married well.
Vic Padovani, the one son, possessively spoilt by his
mother and bullied by his father, had gone into the
army, where his extreme good looks had not made his
life easy. He was now back, assistant manager and
general dogsbody.

Coffin always enjoyed a visit there. It brought back
for him too that pre-war world he was to find again,
as well as the new one he was looking for. Another
brick in his wall.

THE ENTIRE Theatre Royal company sat round a long
table, drinking coffee and eating the sort of sandwiches that The Padovani produced at this hour of
evening. They probably had horsemeat in them. Or
whalemeat, someone said, because they did taste fishy.

It had been a bad day for food at Mrs Lorimer's,
perhaps she had quarrelled with the butcher, so that
Coffin and Alex Rowley were glad to eat at all.

Stella waved to them as they came in. 'Join us, dar-
lings.'

She was in high spirits. One play, *An Inspector
Calls*, had ended and *Candida* would shortly open.
She was sure of a success. She called down the table to
stage manager Chris. 'By the way, why do we have to
have a perambulator on scene for the first act of *Candida*?'

She made a production of the word perambulator, stretching out the syllables, modulating the vowels.

Joan pricked up her ears, recognizing the echoes of Rachel Esthart's unique voice. She hoped Rachel was not going to be too much for the girl. It had always been a gamble sending the child there. Good for Rachel, taking her out of herself, giving her an interest, but bad for Stella? It would be fine if Stella could take all Rachel had to offer without getting swallowed up by her.

Joan's anxieties extended to Eddie Kelly whose effect on young women she knew only too well. And not only women.

'Parson's house. There would be children around. Albie thought it in character. Makes a point,' said Chris.

'I thought it was because we happened to have a pram around.'

'There is an element of that in it. It was Widow Twankey's pram in our Christmas *Aladdin*. Eddie pushed.'

Yes, Eddie would make a good Widow Twankey, thought Stella, having just the right mixture of malice and ruthlessness.

Eddie grinned at her from across the table. 'You should have seen my boots.'

'Nothing to do with left-overs,' said Joan sharply. 'With Albie, it's an aesthetic matter. And I'd like to know who's been messing about with the pram. Filthy. Poor Chris has had a terrible time with it.' Joan was careful with her properties. 'I wish you lot would remember how hard it is to get things. You can't just go out and buy them.'

'There's a war on,' they chorused.

Watching them, Coffin thought what a closed world they were. The death of the girl, her murder, did not really touch them. Today they had played a success so they were happy, tomorrow they might play a failure, then they would be sad.

Coffin had a sudden vivid inner picture of Eddie Kelly as Widow Twankey wearing big boots, pushing his pram. Eddie acting his head off. Wasn't there a murderer who had pushed his victim in a pram?

The Padovani waitress, affectionately known as Shirley Temple because of her tightly curled pale hair, planted a plate of sandwiches in front of Coffin. 'That's your lot. Beef's off now. But I can do you spam. If we've got any bread.'

Bread was in short supply. Spam, however, at the moment, was plentiful but on 'points'.

Chris wandered across from the theatre table, sat down opposite Coffin, and took a sandwich. 'I'm starving. They eat like wolves, that lot, don't they, but never put on an ounce. Hard work being an actor, I suppose.' He sounded detached as if being a musician and stage manager put him in a different category.

Coffin ate a sandwich, better get one quick before the wolves moved over here too. Alex muttered something about talking to Stella and crossed to the big table.

Chris took the opportunity to talk.

'About the girl that was found in the river. Just a kid?'

Coffin nodded.

'I know one of the reporters on the *Mercury*. He told me the girl had one long fingernail on a little finger.'

'That's right.'

'Gave me an idea. Could have played the guitar. Guitar-players like to have a bit of extra length in that way. Might help identify her. Try the Music Conservatory on the hill. They might have heard of her. Or a school. She might teach music.'

'Thanks. I'll do that. Have you told anyone else?' Chris shook his head.

'Well, don't.'

He drank some coffee, which was strong and hot, the coffee at The Padovani restaurant was always good. Mrs Lorimer provided a paler, weaker brew. He'd be away from his attic as soon as he could find a place.

'You don't know a girl who plays the guitar?'

'I did know one,' said Chris softly. 'Played with her once in a little orchestra.'

'When?'

'Our last panto,' said Chris reluctantly. 'Christmas 1945. I did the music. An economy effect. I was just out of the army.'

'Aladdin?'

'That's right. Ask Joan and Albie. They should have some record. They paid her wages. She was a bit stage-struck, poor kid. Hung around.'

'When did you last see her?'

Chris shook his head. 'Can't remember. Not for some time. Ask Joan and Albie.'

Coffin said calmly: 'What you're really telling me, Chris, is that you were a friend of the dead girl.'

'Might have been.'

'You took your time getting out with it.'

'You try doing it better sometimes. It's not a thing you want to hurry with when the kid's been murdered. Anyway, I'm not sure.'

'There's an easy way to find out. You'll have to come down to the mortuary. See if you can identify her.'

'I was afraid you'd say that.' His hand trembled as he picked up his coffee. The cup rattled against the saucer.

'What was her name?'

'Lorna. Lorna Beezley.'

'I'll fix for you to get a look.'

'Lovely,' muttered Chris. 'I'll be looking forward to it.'

Stella came across, a glass in her hand. 'You're looking serious. Not to be. This is a party, my party, I'm celebrating.'

True child of the theatre, she could separate herself from the outside world in which murder could happen to a girl her own age, to concentrate on her own true world.

'We've got two bottles of wine out of Ma Padovani and you're to have a glass and wish me luck. I'm going to be the Lady in a masque we are going to put on before the King and Queen: when they come. Did you know they were coming?'

Coffin nodded: he knew. The royal visit, bringing with it, as it would, any number of spivs, pickpockets and con men, was adding to the work of the police. Just for a moment Stella seemed too bright, too heartless.

'Don't judge her,' muttered Chris. 'It's that old witch she's living with. God, I hate the theatre sometimes. It's so blood-sucking.'

Stella was talking to Alex, then to Joan and Albie. Her little summer dress, tight-waisted, with a full skirt, her hair cropped short like a boy's. For *Candida* she would wear a wig.

'Mrs Esthart? Don't you like her? I've only met her once, but I thought her quite a character.'

'One day I'll tell you why I dislike her. No. I'll tell you now.' Chris seemed high, he'd had a bit to drink. The Padovanis' rough red wine (made in their backyard in a bucket, according to legend) was powerful stuff. 'She ruined my old man. He wrote plays. Good plays. They got produced. Directors liked him. Then Rachel Esthart turned thumbs down on him. Said he was old hat, passé. People believed her. He died of cancer a year later, and he was still talking about her. Trying to defend himself.' He was still looking at Stella.

Half way across the room Eddie Kelly slapped her, put his arm round her and kissed her bare shoulder.

It was a loving and intimate gesture, delivered with style, as if he was putting a label on a piece of his property.

Chris stood up abruptly. 'I'll be off.' He got himself into his raincoat. Outside a cold summer rain was falling. 'How's Lorimer's suiting you?'

'I'll be making a change. Nothing against the place; I just feel like making a move.'

'Everyone does. You'd be surprised how many get stuck. Say goodbye to Stella for me.'

'I'll be in touch about the other thing,' added Coffin after him.

Without a backward look Chris was gone. None too steadily, either.

'Drunk again,' said Joan sadly, to no one in particular.

Coffin moved his seat to sit next to her. 'Do you know a girl called Lorna Beezley.'

'Not really, dear.' She too was mildly sozzled.

'She worked for you. In the orchestra at the pantomime.'

'We didn't have an orchestra. Just a trio.'

'She was in the trio, then.'

Joan looked troubled. 'Why are you asking? No, don't tell me, I can guess. I saw Chris talking to you. He's in love with Stella now, you know. He has these things. Love is all.'

'Can you give me Lorna Beezley's address?'

'If I've still got it. I'm not a great keeper of paperbits.'

Coffin waited, confident something was coming.

'Oh, all right. I expect I can find it. I do know she worked in a nursery school in the day. Taught infants. But she was theatre-mad. Hung about all the time, even when she wasn't working. I didn't like her much, but I do hope she isn't—'

'You didn't like her?'

'She was so nasty about the children, dear. A flip little tongue, she had.'

Joan drained her glass of wine. 'Well now, want a run-down on the whole company? I can tell who's sleeping with whom.'

Coffin was silent.

'Oh, shoot me instead,' she said.

'You've been very helpful.'

'I had to be, hadn't I? But don't worry Albie. He's got enough on his mind.'

Her husband was always protected by Joan.

'Don't tell anyone but we're bankrupt, pretty well. Pay the wages. Just. Thank God for clothes rationing, it does keep the cost down.'

'She *was* drunk.

'But we'll come through. Eddie's going, damn him. Going into the new Rattigan. But Stella's a great draw, so thank God.'

Despair and hope, the theatrical see-saw.

Stella was talking to Shirley the waitress, arranging to have the bill on tick. From what Coffin now knew, the look of doubt in Shirley's face was justified.

'I dunnow. Mrs P. always says: No credit. Especially to theatricals.'

The two girls stood side by side. Stella's summer dress was skimpy and short, her skin gleamed. Shirley in her blouse and tight black skirt looked over-dressed, but she fitted into her uniform beautifully.

She was wearing thin, transparent stockings. Stella's legs were bare, nylons not yet having come her way. They were black market material, unless you had an American friend. Shirley looked at though she could have both. A nice girl but not fussy.

'A week to pay and I'll tell you where they're getting some Arden lipstick in.'

'Where?'

'Purvis's in Powis Street.'

They'll all have gone by the time I get there.'

'I'll let you have mine. And two tickets for *Candida*.' Shirley was a keen theatre-goer, although Bernard Shaw was not her favourite choice.

'I'll be shot,' she said, giving way.

'Actually I've got a lipstick in my purse now. I'll give it you.'

The girl's face lit up with joy; she held out her hand.

On the way home to Angel House, Stella said: 'I'm happy, you see. And you have to do good things when you're happy.'

She put her arm through his, and Coffin put his hand around hers: it seemed only polite.

'I'll tell you why I'm happy. Not just the Masque, although that's part. Rachel is getting Nick Devizes down to watch me. He's casting a new play. He might want me. In fact, I think he will. I'm right for the part. It's my big chance.'

Poor old Joan and Albie, poor old Repertory Company, lucky little Stella. If it came off.

He bent down and kissed her. For a moment her lips held back, then they parted gently and she kissed back.

'I do love you, Stella.' It was the sort of thing people said, people like him at that age and that way of life.

'No, you don't, but that was nice.'

They walked on.

'You don't have to tell lies to me. I can kiss you without being in love. I don't want to be loved. Love can rot things up. Look at Rachel Esthart. She fell in love, married, had that child and it ruined her in the end. She knows it now, but it's too late.'

The murder was casting its bleak shadow backwards and forwards, forcing from Stella this blunt honesty.

'I think she's giving up that son of hers. Stopping believing he's alive, I mean. That card on the body sort of shook her. Who wants a son like that? She doesn't. She's not mad really, you know, just got into a state. A bit obsessive, but aren't we all?'

'I could be,' he said, and kissed her again.

Behind them the door of Angel House swung open silently, a black note giving upon a greater darkness.

Stella gave a scream. Coffin drew her to him, covering her eyes. 'Don't look, love, don't look.'

TWO HOURS LATER he walked back to Mrs Lorimer's establishment.

There was blood on his hands, on his suit, his best and only, the demob special. 'Damn.' Considering what he had been through, it was a moderate explosion.

He had held Stella in his arms while Florence appeared with a bucket and newspaper. It was she who had opened the door.

He shielded Stella into the house, pushing her off to see if Mrs Esthart was all right, then went back himself to take over. He took the bird down from the door where it had been nailed by its wings, then carried it off on a spade to bury. On the doorstep were the entrails of the creature in a pool of blood. He ordered Florrie off to make some coffee and cleaned up. Not a nice job.

Rachel Esthart slept through it all. She had not been disturbed by the banging on the door which had brought Florrie out.

He held Stella in his arms as he said goodbye.

'I thought it was Rachel at first, when you wouldn't let me look. Then I thought Punchy Pooh.'

Punchy was Rachel's dog.

'A bird, only a bird.'

'What sort of bird?'

'A seagull.' Seagulls were plentiful around the river, natural scavengers. This one had probably been dead or dying. Plenty of blood, though.

Stella gave a gasp and drew away. 'A seagull? As good as saying an actress. Tchekhov's play called *The Seagull* is all about a girl who is an actress: Nina. One of Rachel's biggest successes was as Nina.' She put her hands over her face. 'Oh.'

With foreboding he said: 'And what is the play you are being considered for?'

'*The Seagull*. Nina.'

IT WOULD BE VERY EASY to love Stella. Real love, not just kissing love. But he wouldn't do it. He was just like Stella herself, eyes forward, he wouldn't take time off to fall in love—when he heard people say Stella was becoming a slave to Rachel Esthart he knew it wasn't love: Stella was pursuing her own end. Stella was slave only to Stella.

Even as he decided this he realized that whatever his mind thought of it, his body had other views, and that he was strongly and perhaps permanently in love with Stella Pinero.

As he plodded home many different thoughts jostled in his mind. All mental roads were crowded with traffic. It reminded him of a scene during the war when he had sat in an armoured car with tanks, jeeps, cars and foot soldiers all jammed in one solid mass. Then all the elements in the jam had sorted themselves out and streamed away to their appointed positions. After the clear came the battle.

The light was still on in Alex's basement room, but he ignored it. He wasn't going to talk to Alex.

No signs of Mrs Lorimer, one hardly ever saw her although her presence was strongly felt.

There was a note for him from her on the hall table: 'Mr Coffin, you have not given me your points this month. I cannot give you a cooked breakfast unless you do.'

Dry toast, then? But even bread was rationed.

Policemen got extra rations, extra points. It was heavy work being a policeman.

Lady Olivia was quiet behind her door. He wondered if he'd ever see her, he never had yet, although he'd heard singing and distant bangings. Could she be the tall, prim woman with an Edwardian pompadour hair style he saw at supper sometimes?

He climbed on up to the attic. From the window he could see the lights of London; he opened the window to catch the breeze blowing across Greenwich Park. A ship hooted as it went towards the estuary on a rising tide, and a passing ship replied. They were talking to each other.

Out there was the murderer of the girl, who now had a name and a bit of character for him to play with.

He had felt the presence of the murderer before, now he thought he knew his stance, the way he moved.

Aggressive, quick-witted, wayward. A proper bugger.

As he looked down from his eyrie he was frightened. The killer seemed that much closer.

He had another problem on his mind. He had to scratch around for a second to recall what it was: then he remembered Aunt Gert's little legacy. His unknown sibling. But suddenly he realized he would know that one's stance too. It would be like his own. They shared the same parent. He might know him or her by sight. It was a thought.

And somehow, cheering.

FOUR

THE FEET OF THE MURDERER

DID SHE WALK or was she pushed? That was the thought that Coffin asked himself as he walked to work that next morning.

They had the forensic report in now and knew she had been strangled, then stabbed while moribund, then dropped in the river. The scientists were not clear as yet as to the weapon itself, but they could say it had a sharp point, a tapered blade sharp on both sides.

He took a quick look at Angel House as he passed. All fair and square there. No blood, no bird, its war-battered face looked as usual. Its time to get its windows in must come soon. The Lorimer hotel had glass again.

It was Alex Rowley's late duty, and he had left him sleeping. Good luck to him and breakfast: one strange, small, yellowish egg, origin doubtful but probably a hen.

The first thing to do was to tell Tom Banbury about the possible identification of the dead girl. He would follow up with the story of the dead bird, crucified on the door of Angel House.

This morning the episode seemed even more bizarre and no less frightening.

Angel House was quite a sight, he thought. Not exactly cobwebs and dust-sheets but very nearly. Lots of clocks, all over the house, and not one going. Not Mrs Esthart's room, though, that was all glass, bronze and white silk. Stella said it was designed by a man called Lobel from Paris and was famous. *Nearly* clean, he thought. It was no good pretending he was enjoying this investigation: it was a savage introduction to the job. Mentally he was dictating his *aide-mémoire*:

Mrs Esthart in a pink satin quilted robe with fluffy sleeves. A bit grubby round the edges. She had Punchy Pooh with her; I think he's a Peke but hard to be sure as he was buried in satin, except for two eyes and snout.

Stella's quite right: Esthart's coming out of her missing-son syndrome. I caught the gleam of hard, cold sanity in her eyes. Especially when she made sure all doors were locked behind me.

Anyone could get in that house, though. Wide open. Emotionally as well; those women were vulnerable.

Angel House and its precious occupant, darling Stella, off his mind for the moment, he hurried down the hill to take a look at Greenwich Pier. He had half an hour in which to give a quick survey to see if there were any signs that the girl's body had gone into the river there. Then a tram to work; he enjoyed a tram ride, especially if he went on the top to sit on the prow as on a galleon. You could sit there to smoke and not envy the King himself.

He was out so early that a haze still hung over the city. He had time to walk across the heath, down Maze Hill towards the Wren buildings and the river. London lay stretched out majestically before him.

What a city to pillage, the old Prussian General had said.

A few workmen were standing waiting for a tram at the corner of King William Walk and Nelson Road. A milk-cart pulled by an elderly horse trundled past him into Romney Street. England's great sailors of the past are well represented in Greenwich street names in a manner which Dutch King William might not have appreciated had he lived to see them, any more than Charles de Gaulle did when recently given the chance.

He walked along the pier, which is short and broad, lined with a few benches. At the further end, with its back to the entrance, there was a wooden booth which had sold chocolate and ice-cream in peacetime. 'Fry's Chocolate Creams' proclaimed a faded advertisement, 'Twopence a bar', and another offered 'Eldorado ice-cream sticks'.

He went inside, it smelt sour and it was grubby, but there were cigarette ends and scraps of newspaper on the floor, signs of human habitation. People used this place.

He went out, taking another quick look around the pier. Then soon a turn to the left to walk along a path which ran a hundred yards along the water's edge and where iron railings bordered either side. At intervals sturdy flights of stone steps went down to the water. There were gates, but unlocked.

He did not know what he was looking for, just a feeling perhaps. Or just to see for himself.

He had no doubt that other policemen had walked this path already, looking and searching. He wanted to understand. Presumptuous of him, possibly; he guessed that this might be the worst sin a young detective could commit. But he intended to commit it.

He lingered at the flights of steps, three flights in all, all giving easy access to the water. You could get at these steps from two directions: from Trafalgar Road through Park Walk and from King William's Walk.

A picture of a body being pushed there in some conveyance came into his mind. Pushed like a baby in a pram? Or possibly tugged along on some improvised sledge. There was a pram in the theatre.

Who would see late at night? In London someone probably would. Except that it was dark here at night, the street lamps still not working after the war, people might not linger.

On the other hand a couple could walk here, like lovers, close and warm, with only the murderer knowing what lay ahead.

Stand by the steps and embrace in the dark, then be killed and pushed into the water for the river to deal with.

Two pictures of a death. One with the girl being pushed already dead, and the other her walking to that fate.

The girl must have been wearing shoes, had probably been carrying a handbag, but neither had been found.

As he walked back along the river path he noticed that where the brick walls supporting the path and pier made an angle, and there were three such places, here rubbish collected. He saw bottles and tins, empty cigarette boxes and assorted rubbish swirling and bouncing in the tide.

He stared down looking for something interesting but finding nothing.

He walked back, then caught a tram. On the tram, sitting on the top, he had time to think. He did not want to believe he *knew* the killer, knew him as a person. He wished him to be anonymous, a figure plucked from the crowd by a single act of violence like the killer of the Shepherd woman. But more and more as the perspective lines in the picture he saw centred upon Angel House and the Theatre Royal, he felt that the murderer was going to be a man known to him.

He could think of two possibilities. Two men worked at the Theatre Royal and had links with Rachel Esthart.

One was Edward Kelly, and the other was Chris Mackenzie. Chris had already expressed a strong dislike of Rachel Esthart. Edward Kelly had loved her once and been rejected. He might have hatred burning inside him.

This was not going to be a case where a tight alibi would eliminate any man, because there was no exact time for the killing.

At some time, about two days before her body had
been found, and probably shortly before her body had
gone into the water, she had been strangled and then
stabbed and deeply mutilated. She had not been raped.

There was a further complication.

A murderer who called himself Rachel Esthart's son
had despatched her on her way.

You could reject this idea of a living, murderous son
or you could accept it.

If you accepted the son as still around and ready to
kill, then you had to look for someone in a certain age-
group.

Chris Mackenzie fitted, but Eddie Kelly did not.
Names to throw around; there would be others.

At the back of his mind was what he called his
'dark' thought which bore directly upon his private
and professional life, questioning all his deeply held
beliefs about the relationship between men and their
loyalties. That thought would not go away.

And if there was no son, and someone was playing
games, then your choice was wide open again.

As the tram bounced along to its destination, John
Coffin blinked in the sunshine. 'It will all come together,' he said aloud.

The passenger next to him looked at him in alarm,
then moved away to another seat. There were a lot of
lunatics loose in London just now. This passenger was
not anxious to run across them. Just demobbed, this
passenger was starting work in a new job that day; he
was going to work for W. J. Clarke, butcher, of Mel-
ville Street, Lewisham, with whom there was a long-

standing family connection. Not a job for life, but it would do for a start. So no lunatics, please.

Coffin's emptying stomach rumbled as he got off the train and hurried in to see his boss. He could still taste that breakfast egg, the ghost of it still about his mouth. It was an egg that seemed to have come a long way, and had a hard journey of it. No egg to forget.

But he felt strong enough to face Tom Banbury, and this made his step confident and happy.

MRS LORIMER HAD HEARD her lodger depart, and noted that all policemen seemed to walk with that firm confident ring. Her two young detectives certainly did. Quite different from the way soldiers walked.

That was Mr Rowley on the stairs now. A nice young man, easier to know than Mr Coffin, who sometimes seemed to have an abstracted way with him as if he was looking right through you and out the other side, and seeing something quite different.

From her contacts in the police force she knew that Tom Banbury was quite troubled about them both. 'My difficult youngsters,' he called them. The first new intake since the war and they had their own ideas. It was the Labour Government's fault. Young policemen had not been so before the war.

Not that Tom Banbury was an easy man himself, never had been, too buttoned up and reserved, the more so since his wife had been killed. Drink, it was called, and probably there *was* drink too, but much else besides. Unstable. His father had been badly wounded in the last war and kept a bayonet on the wall

in his bedroom to prove it. Lilly Lorimer had seen the
bayonet, still there on his deathbed. It was bad for a
boy to grow up looking at a bayonet.

As with the breakfast, that was the government's
fault too. Britain had won the war, hadn't it?

And there was Lady Olivia. No mistaking her tread
either. She'd fall from top to bottom one day.

'No, Lady Olivia,' she said firmly. 'There is nothing the matter with your egg. You're lucky to have
one. It's not your turn for an egg this week at all. *Next*
week you get your rationed egg. This one is off the
ration. The butcher let me have a dozen Chinese eggs
off the ration.'

Distantly she heard Lady Olivia muttering something about her butcher, and bacon.

'Two ounces, Lady Olivia. Two ounces, and you ate
it all yesterday.'

STELLA WAS SITTING at her make-up box, extracting
one by one the materials for her face as Candida; she
had tried several faces, never getting the one she
wanted. She was not an actress who liked to appear
with her face as God made it. Every time she wanted
to create something different.

In this she was at odds with Rachel Esthart, who
had been content to project herself, naturally and
powerfully. But then Rachel was a beauty, and always
would be.

Not for the first time, Stella wondered what the Lost
Boy had been like, what the father had been like, and

also the lover who had precipitated the final explosion.

People did gossip about it. Albie and Joan did, so did Edward Kelly, but only to a point. They closed up just when it got interesting.

Her hand outlined her lips, still shaking. This might have been due to the strong draughts that blew all around her on that cold summer. The Theatre Royal was a charming theatre but it was ramshackle and cold. One day its bomb-damage grant would come through and then it would be refurbished, when pieces of its history would be tucked away. The dusty scenery from a forgotten production of *Swan Lake* (Albie and Joan had briefly dabbled in ballet brought down from London) which was propped against the wall in Stella's dressing-room would go. As would the tea-chest full of decaying costumes left over from the two seasons of Great Classics of the Theatre dating from well before the war. As it was, people fell over the past, walked into it, cursed it, and generally ignored it. When it was gone it would be too late, then someone would write a book about it.

'Stella?'

It was Bluebell Harrison, a junior member of the cast, a character actress in the making. After a short initial period of jealousy, Stella and the rest of the cast had established a friendly, cosy relationship, as is the way with theatricals. A company that is quarrelling is on the way to disaster. The rest of them knew that Stella had something going with Eddie Kelly, and probably with someone else as well, but they were not moralists and did not hold it against her. They warmed themselves against her vitality. In short, she was popular. Bluebell bore her no animosity for wresting away Edward on whom she had staked a mild claim, recognizing that Eddie was probably too much for her anyway.

'I nipped down to Powis Street this morning and got myself an Arden lipstick. Six shillings and ninepence, and pillar-box red the only colour. Doesn't suit me but I got it, anyway.'

'Oh, good.' Stella was still improving her Candida face. She squinted at it.

'And if I can't wear it then I can trade it for something. Chloe's got some nail varnish that's quite pretty.' A good deal of bartering went on in the company. A box of face-powder for a pair of stockings, a lipstick against a bottle of scent. 'Anyway, what I came for: here's a letter.'

Stella received a letter from her best friend Kay and slipped it under her make-up box. When Bluebell had gone, Stella got it out to read. Then she started a reply.

Stella wrote:

You are quite right, Kay, love, I am nervous of my lover. Not that he is my lover. Not completely. I wouldn't dare. I think it would blow the top of my head off. His too, probably.

Her hand shook. The episode last night had frightened her more than she had admitted even to John

Coffin. Later, she was to see her violent lover as a killer. Already she had sensed the narrow margin between pleasure and pain. Then she wrote:

> I will tell you the name of the person I am afraid of, then if anything happens to me you will know.

The Theatre Royal was disintegrating so rapidly that flakes of plaster, rust and paint were always depositing themselves all over everyone who came there, so that all who came to the theatre went away with a bit of it on them.

Now a flake of plaster fell on to Stella's letter, but she was so used to such a deposit that she flicked it away with a finger and sealed the flap. A little shred of paint and a powdering of rust were secreted inside with the name of a man.

Stella did not send the letter to Kay, she wasn't sure she meant to even, but by writing down the name she had taken away a little of the man's force.

It was a primitive way of thinking, but actresses can be very primitive sometimes.

She put the letter in her make-up box, a little time-bomb (a word with which Hitler had made them familiar) waiting to explode.

JOHN COFFIN SAW that Tom Banbury was already at his desk, sitting with his shoulders hunched in that way he had as if the weight of the world was on his shoulders.

His room had a strong character all of its own which Tom Banbury had not dispelled. In its earliest days this part of the old school had housed Mixed Infants. Tom had the Headmistress's room and the ghost of this long-dead lady made itself felt.

Try as he would, he had never been able to efface a disposition in the furniture of the room to arrange itself like a schoolroom. His desk *would* assume the air of a desk and the chairs arrange themselves in rows.

He was an unhappy man and looked it. The sight of Detective-Constable Coffin did not cheer him. He had worries he was not prepared to share. And he was none too pleased to see John Coffin at that time. But he was a polite man; he let the young detective have his say: the girl's fingernail, her possible identity, the ghost of the seagull.

For a moment Coffin thought Tom Banbury had not heard him: he started again. 'Chris Mackenzie...'

'Yes. I heard. The pathologists pointed out the fingernail. We have an identification. She has been positively identified.' He went on: 'You were right, as you said.' He sounded absent, as if his deeper thoughts were elsewhere. 'You should have reported the bird last night. Nasty. I'll go up to see Mrs Esthart myself.'

'She'd be glad.'

'But we're out of it now. Not altogether, naturally. There'll be plenty to do. We've asked for help from the Yard. You'll meet the man this morning. Andy Warwick, Chief Inspector Warwick. You'll like him.'

'I see, sir.' And this was true, for not only had they this murder to deal with, but the preparations for the royal visit to cope with. In addition, there were all the usual items like the goods going missing from the docks that were turning up on stalls in Woolwich market. Someone (it was Alex) had to deal with that.

'I've got plenty on my plate. Quite a dish.'

It was so unusual for him to make a joke of any sort, that John Coffin hardly took in what he meant, then he realized: the Shepherd child.

'Have there...? I mean...' He stopped. How could you say out aloud: What other bits—leg, arm or other members of that poor kid—have turned up? 'Any more news, sir?'

'Yes. You've got it. A hand this time. A very small hand.'

One way and another there were so many bones disturbed over London then. In 1917 a German Zeppelin had exploded, tossing one of the crew into the Abbey Woods beyond Woolwich (the Abbey long since gone) where he had been waiting to be found ever since. Some thousand years before an Anglo-Saxon girl had been lost and had been working her way to the surface of the land since then. She was just about ready to be found. In 1940 a land-mine blew all the occupants of an omnibus far and wide. Not all the bodies were found. Bits of them travelled too far. It had been a hard war, but the Lions had played on at Millwall, and Charlton at the Valley.

'A tiny hand,' repeated Tom Banbury. He looked down at his own hand. A minute tremble began near the knuckles, then spread down to the fingertip. A tiny movement, but observable.

He hates all this, thought Coffin. He absolutely bloody hates all this.

All police officers hate the murder of a child, but Coffin picked up something else as well, which at the moment he could not name, but it felt like shame.

It was at that moment that John Coffin knew that something was wrong.

He looked away. You don't want to catch your superior out in a private emotion, it's not the way to get on in the world. And, if you are like John Coffin, you don't enjoy it anyway.

From outside came the sound of doors banging, a voice talking cheerful, and a lower voice answering.

Dander and Warwick, like a pair of cross-talk comedians, had arrived.

IT WAS IMPOSSIBLE not to like Dander, he had such style. John Coffin sat there drinking in the details of his appearance and behaviour. The jacket loose and unbuttoned as if the muscles and energy of the man had burst it apart. The crisply curling hair, cut short and greying at the temples but long at the back, was in character. He made his own style.

What a beast, he thought. Will I be like that when I'm forty?

Was Dander forty? About that, probably, must have been in the forces somewhere but it was hard to see as what. Impossible as a private, he would have been much worse as an officer. He was an army in himself.

Coffin admired him immensely.

Inspector Warwick was another case altogether: young, hard, tough, and nasty. But at the same time you could tell he was reliable. Trustworthy but bloody, the worst combination.

They were all crowded into the room that had been the art-room in the days of the school. Never a large room, it was now full of large men. Present were the men from Scotland Yard, Warwick and his sergeant. The pair were flanked by Dander and Banbury.

The rest of them, the whole team of men who would be working on the river case, sat where they could. Coffin sat next to Alex Rowley who had arrived late, breathless.

Tom Banbury had spoken, Dander had spoken, Warwick had spoken. The rest of them had listened. A bit like going into battle. But at least they knew their jobs. A roster of duties for the day, the week ahead.

Alex was to stay with Tom Banbury working on the Shepherd case. He pulled a sour face at Coffin and shrugged.

John Coffin would work with Inspector Warwick, as part of his team, but mostly based in the Greenwich office collating reports. 'A filing job. I'm a bloody clerk,' he muttered resentfully to Alex.

'It'll keep your feet dry.'

A heavy rain was now falling outside.

Warwick delivered a brief summary. 'The victim's name is Lorna Beezley. She was an unmarried girl of twenty-three, a schoolteacher, living at 23 Catherine Street, Greenwich. She had no family. She had been identified by her landlady who had reported her missing. Also, by the headmaster of the Hook Street School where she taught in the Infant Department.'

Dead silence in the room, but outside an earthmoving machine was groaning away in the bomb-site next to the school as it prepared the ground for the new estate.

'She was murdered by strangulation, then mutilated, the genitalia attacked. She was then put in the river. She was dead when she went in.'

'How strangled?' someone asked.

'Manually.'

The chap had strong hands, thought Coffin, who soon would start thinking about the murderer's hands. He looked at his own, broad and thick. But Warwick was going on:

'The river police think she went in the water just before the tide turned in the early morning of May 12th. Greenwich pier and Convoy Wharf were likely points of entry.'

Alex Rowley: 'I could have told him that.'

'You probably did, it was in your report, wasn't it?'

Warwick had more to say.

'We have no strong lead to her killer, but he is out there in the population somewhere and we will bloody well find him. That's an order.' He enumerated what they had to do, handing out tasks efficiently like a croupier dealing out the cards. 'All contacts to be flushed out and talked to. All boyfriends, girlfriends, all the people she worked with, the people where she lodged. Her school and the theatre are vital. Do the

Theatre Royal in Nelson Street. She'd played in the orchestra.'

So they'd got on to that, too? Edward Kelly and Chris Mackenzie were names to Warwick, as well. There was nothing Coffin had that was original.

Except his own dark thoughts.

Warwick said: 'Any questions?'

Coffin put up a hand. 'Sir, she'd have had a hand-bag and shoes. Perhaps gloves. We haven't found them.'

'Right. You've got yourself a job.' Warwick gave him a quick, assessing stare; Dander smiled. No ex-pression appeared on Tom Banbury's face. 'Check what she had at her school and lodgings. You know the address. Don't think I'd overlooked it, though.' Dander's smile broadened.

Coffin was pleased. I've got myself an out, he thought. I was pushed on the edge, but I'm crawling back in. And I don't mind if I get my feet wet.

'Any more questions?' Warwick was brisk.

There were none. Warwick's face precluded it, somehow.

Warwick said: 'In my view this is a straight sex crime. The girl may have known her killer. Or he may have been a stranger. You will all have heard of the so-called message found on her. My opinion is that you should ignore it. In my view it is a joke.'

As they went out Coffin thought he heard Dander saying something to Banbury about a pet-shop and private zoo in Greenwich Hythe Street that had been bombed silly. Any pets there must have had a rough time.

HOOKEY STREET, he was going to Hookey Street. Back to Hookey Street.

You leave a school at fourteen, shake its chalk dust from your feet, and swear never to see the place again.

A war and nearly ten years later, you go back to investigate a murder.

Could Mr Poole still be Headmaster? No, that would make him about ninety. Wait a minute, though. He might have looked like a battered old lizard ten years ago, but he had probably been well under fifty. Old men were not appointed to be heads of schools like Hook Street. Such men had to be tough, physically and mentally. Poole had been tough, John Coffin's bottom had borne witness to the power of old Poole's right arm.

Hook Street School had not been changed for the better by the war. The asphalt playground still contained the great square water container put up in 1940 to hold water for another fire-bomb raid. It was empty of water now but full of litter. It smelt as though the cats of Hook Street used it too.

The ground-floor of Hook Street school had great ARP signs in white paint all over the walls. It had been both an Air-raid Wardens' post and an Auxiliary Fire Service station.

In the school playground was the wooden hut which had housed the infant class taught by Lorna Beezley.

Coffin looked up to the floor where Senior Boys had once held sway. Two kids looked down at him from a window.

'THERE'S A YOUNG MAN crossing the playground,' said Miss Jeffries to Miss Arden. They were in the staffroom, the only occupants since the rest of the staff had responded to the end-of-break bell.

'Ah.' Miss Arden came to look. 'Well, don't be too hopeful, dear. He hasn't come for us.'

Miss Jeffries took another look. 'He's a policeman. You know why he's come, don't you?'

Just before school closed yesterday afternoon two policemen in plain clothes had called. They had all been late home. ITMA night too. Oh, the pain of missing Tommy Handley.

'But we've told all we know.'

'Not quite all, have we?'

'All I did was to keep quiet,' said Helen Jeffries slowly. 'I thought we agreed.'

'I think we were wrong.'

'She's dead. Poor child.'

'All the same.'

'Couldn't be any connection,' muttered Helen Jeffries. 'I don't think I shall want to say.'

Alma Arden took another look out of the window through which she got a clear vision of John's uplifted face. She drew in a quick breath.

'Do you remember years ago in Junior Mixed School a lad with auburn hair, ginger almost, who stole all the wood from the Senior Boys' woodwork

class because he said he was building an ark to escape
with?'

'Do I not? He said he'd join the police when he got
older and be like Sherlock Holmes.'

'I think he's made his ambition. A bit of it, anyway. I must say I always thought he'd go to prison.'

They stood there looking out of the window, ignor-
ing the increasing noise of their neglected classes.

THE FAMILIAR NOISE of school greeted John Coffin's
ears as he went into Hook Street School. He felt he
knew his way around. Apart from any memories of
the building, it was almost identical to the one in
which he now worked.

The only difference from the old days was that Mr
Poole had given place to Miss Swann, a tall, slender
woman who was now interviewing him. To Coffin it
felt that way around.

'Mr Poole retired in 1939. He came back to work in
1940 as head of Basco Road School. We were very
short of men teachers. The school got a direct hit from
a flying-bomb in 1944.' She answered his unspoken
question. 'Yes, killed at once.'

Just about the same time as Coffin himself was being exploded. Not a coincidence, exactly, but not a
coupling of their situations that either party would
have predicted all those years ago.

'I'm sorry.' But it wasn't true; he was not sorry.
Suddenly he was aware of a lightening of the spirit, a
figure that had loomed in the background for years
had leapt off his back and disappeared. Old Poole was

gone, taking a bit of Coffin's past with him, and glad
to see it go.

'Of course you have my permission to talk to the
staff, but everything was told to the investigating officers yesterday. I'm really surprised to get another
visit.' Time to waste, her manner implied.

'Special questions,' Coffin mumbled. 'Something
a bit different. About her clothes. I'd like to speak to
the women on your staff.'

'There are no men. We have no boys in the school.
During the war when the ARP took over the ground
floor, the Infants went up to the top floor and the
Senior Boys went round to Basco Street.'

Evacuation had briefly thinned out the school population of Greenwich Wick and Greenwich Hythe in
the autumn of 1939, but the sturdy inhabitants had
soon come pouring back to sit out the Blitz and most
of the flying-bombs and rockets, too. Anything was
better than country living.

Coffin and Helen Jeffries knew each other at once:
she, of course, pre-warned.

'Miss Judge!'

'Jeffries,' she corrected automatically. She knew her
nickname. She taught a modest amount of English
history, and had expected what she got.

It would be idle to pretend the young detective had
not enjoyed questioning the teaching staff. For the
first time he was in the chair and asking questions.

And getting some answers. Starting with Miss
Swann.

'I can only repeat what I said before. A cotton dress and a cardigan. It was what she usually wore. We all wear the same clothes, more or less.' She shrugged. 'Coupons, utility clothes, we look alike, Mr Coffin. As to her shoes and bag, I expect they were more or less like mine.' She extended a thin ankle with a solid brown brogue shoe. 'And handbags—' She pointed out her one brown leather handbag. 'We can't all find Joyce Wedgies and a matching shoulder-bag.'

When he left her he had been handed a great truth: most women had only one handbag. Whatever had been the fashion in the past, the average woman did not now change her handbag with her outfit.

He knew he'd got news when he saw Helen Jeffries: she was wearing red shoes. He wondered Miss Swann hadn't noticed, but she probably only saw what she expected. Most of the population did that.

'I'd better tell you. It didn't seem important, not a matter of life and death, but now you're asking about her shoes and handbag I must say. She was probably wearing them, after all. An evening out, she'd wear her best shoes.'

She looked down at her own feet, then silently produced a flat red shoulder-bag from a drawer.

'I love pretty things, and we've been starved. Lorna got me this. I paid, but no coupons. She got them from her boyfriend. I suppose they were stolen, black-market. They are export stuff, you see, not meant for us at all. I'm ashamed, I suppose. Only not much,' she ended defiantly. 'I've been bombed and starved for five years, and the peace has come. I want my share of pretty things.'

You and Stella and Rachel Esthart, and most of the women of England. Only people like Miss Swann seemed exempt. 'There won't be any trouble about that,' he said gently. But he had a question. 'Who was the boyfriend?'

'No idea. There wasn't just one, you know. She was always out dancing. Or the theatre. That was her life. Not teaching. And I don't blame her.'

No, nor did John Coffin, but she had twinkled away in her red shoes and never been seen alive again.

HE WENT into the newspaper shop in Hook Street, bought a newspaper, and asked hopefully for some cigarettes.

Under the counter, but some for him because the news-agent liked his face. It fitted Hookey Street (everyone called it Hookey Street).

Coffin's eye fell upon a pile of boys' comic papers. There was a lively picture of a boy in a kilt carrying a magnifying glass. 'Eagle Scott,' ran the caption, 'the laddie detective with the magic eye.'

I could do with some of that, thought our detective.

He read quickly: the laddie was on the track of an escaped Nazi war criminal. The German was fleeing across the highlands of Scotland. A little bit owed to J. Buchan and *The Thirty-Nine Steps* there, he thought.

But he had to know how it went on, and avoiding the newsagent's eye, he bought his copy.

He lit a Woodbine, and went on the top of the tram to smoke, to read, to think.

The next interviews went fast.

'Oh yes,' Lorna's landlady told him. 'Yes, she was wearing red shoes. Loved them. New, you see, no one else had shoes like it. She went dancing in them.'

Another tram, again on the top, this time to Greenwich. Then a walk along the riverside walk.

He could hear the murderer's feet now. Dancing feet. She had walked to her death, he thought, that murdered girl. Gone with her fate as with a lover. Perhaps they had gone dancing first.

Would Rachel Esthart accept a light-footed murderer as her son? Need she be required to? In Coffin's mind this murderer had two possible heads but, as yet, no face.

The tide was well up, lapping against the walls of the pier.

In the right-angle formed between pier and river walk there was a full house of rubbish. Old tins, jam-jars, and beer bottles. Orange peel. Had oranges come back? A long time since he'd seen a free orange.

But beyond the orange, there was a glint of something red.

He leaned over to look. Not a handbag. Might be a shoe.

He took off his jacket, and inched his way in.

A voice from behind hailed him.

'Mister, you mustn't go in the river.' A thin, defiant little boy. 'My gran say's it'll kill you that water. Death, it is.'

The deadly river Thames. Not far wrong, thought Coffin, lowering himself into it. Still, he'd risk it.

FIVE

FOLLOWING THE FEET OF THE MURDERER

THE MURDERER SOON HEARD about the finding of the shoe and was not pleased. Nothing should be found except as he desired. He realized he had been foolish to let the matching shoulder-bag go into the river, although there was no sign of it turning up. Probably it never would. With any luck it was caught somewhere below the water level, never to surface again. Or it had been towed out to sea by a passing ship. As for the shoes, he had not thought of them; they seemed part of the girl.

There was no reason to believe either bag or shoes could be pointed to him, nevertheless there was a loose connection. He should have removed the shoes and lost the bag.

Another time he would be more careful. Once more at least. Then perhaps once again. Then finish. He would have done.

He took the tram that ran towards Deptford, along Creek Road, then down Evelyn Street. A well-bombed area close to the Surrey Docks, not beautiful ever, now shabby and blasted, but containing what he wanted, the place he was looking for.

He got off the tram at the end of Evelyn Street and took a road that led obliquely off it to the docks. In a little sweet shop he used some of his sweet coupons to buy some toffees. Chewing them, he made his way towards Convoy Wharf.

Convoy Wharf was the old cattle delivery point where the cattle ships had come in bearing the living beasts on the hoof ready to be sold in the near-by market and slaughtered. The introduction of refrigerated ships and frozen carcases in the 1920s killed the cattle-market. It was cheaper and easier to carry frozen beef rather than the herds which had to be fed, and watered, across the Atlantic. As Cromwell had said, and the killer believed, stone-dead hath no fellow. Ships bearing paper came into Convoy Wharf now, but there weren't so many these days since newsprint was rationed.

The murderer knew the history of Convoy Wharf, and its connection with slaughter, and had saved it up for special use.

Now he was coming down to take a look round, check it out, as a good soldier might, making notes. Nothing unusual in that, every fit adult male in the country had served in the army.

He took a table in a dock café where a dish of unlovely sausages tumbled and sizzled in a pan all the time. The place was two-thirds full of stevedores, dockers and lightermen. They took no notice of him, he did not stand out, he was in no way remarkable, although they knew he was not one of them.

The murderer did not wear a mask; he always looked exactly himself, knew no other way to do it, but by nature he had been given a face whose planes and angles made him appear calm and without much expression.

As he walked towards Convoy Wharf he did not know that John Coffin was already listening to his tread.

TOM BANBURY KICKED OFF his shoes, removed his socks, then sat back in his armchair. End of day. End of rotten day, a day to make a fool of him. He had known that the bones of the hand found in Greenwich Hythe could not be that of the little Shepherd girl as soon as he looked at them. They didn't look right even to the lay eyes. He had seen enough bones and dead flesh in his day to have an eye for it.

An eye, but not a stomach. He was not in the right job; he should not have been a policeman. What he should have become was not clear to him, possibly a teacher. He liked children. Hated to see them abused.

If the Shepherd child was dead and he found the killer he would be glad to attend his execution. Some people deserved hanging.

The young soldier who had murdered Mrs Shepherd herself would shortly come to trial and if found guilty would be condemned to hang.

Tom Banbury considered the act of execution: he knew what happened, had stood behind the hangman. In Madame Tussaud's.

He stretched out a hand for the bottle of whisky on the floor and poured himself a drink. He would drink until he fell asleep. He was one of those who found comfort in the bottle.

Only Dander knew, because Banbury's sister, Dander's wife, showed this congenital disability. Banbury kept his secret because he only drank when he was sure of being alone. He was almost always alone.

A picture of his wife's body, torn and bleeding, as it must have been after the bomb, floated in front of his eyes. Not her face, he never saw her face, just her naked, blasted body. He had never seen this sight: he had been on a job and away from home when the bomb fell, but he knew how she must have looked. It was peace now, but never peace for him.

This picture always came to him about this time of day because he was at leisure. It was a time he feared and yet loved, the time when he was alone with Elizabeth. Elizabeth was the daughter they would have had, the child his wife had been carrying when she was killed. He had never seen this child, did not truly know its sex, but he was convinced he would have had a daughter. He had lost this child, lost it for ever. This was what fuelled his search for the Shepherd child. He had lost a daughter because of the war; Rachel Esthart had lost a son because she was a drunken slut.

He had to stop thinking that way: it was dangerous. He felt out of control, and God knows he had so many other worries. He was a policeman in the end; it came down to that, God help him.

I won't be beat, he thought, before the bottle took control; I'll get the better of this.

He thought that every time.

STELLA PINERO HAD ONE precious bottle of Arpège scent which she doled out drop by drop. She did not, in fact, like the scent very much, but it was more sophisticated to use it than Chanel No. 5, and even harder to get. The war might be over, but French scent was not easy to come by. Her bottle comforted her. She needed comfort, for her worries were multiplying by the day. Like all actresses, she was emotional, using her emotions, feeding them into the parts she played. She was doing it now with Candida in Shaw's play, and it was leaving her empty. Into this emptiness came fear. She was going to fail as Candida, she was going to be a disaster as The Virgin or The Lady (both names were used) and the Royal Family would be bored. That was probably inevitable.

Her heart sank. Who in this day and age wanted to be either a virgin or a lady?

Now she was meditating an unselfish act, well, fairly unselfish. She was thinking of giving the bottle (trading anyway) to Bluebell, who had no scent, absolutely none.

Stella knew that she was vulnerable to jealousy and spite. She had grabbed the affections of Eddie Kelly, of Chris, and to a lesser extent and granted he was totally loyal to Joan, those of Albie. She had come into the company, and taken everything.

She was now going to fall on her face with Candida, and would be glad of Bluebell's friendship. If she could buy it with a bottle of scent, it was worth it.

Bluebell also had a pair of white shoes and a matching shoulder-envelope which Stella greatly coveted. They didn't fit Bluebell, Stella had seen her limping. Bluebell had big feet for her size, but Stella quite understood why she wore them.

She left her dressing-room and went down the corridor to Bluebell's.

'Bluebell. About those white shoes of yours. Where did you get them?'

She knew Bluebell would not answer, but it was a way in.

IN AN OUTLYING AREA of Leicester there was a small footwear manufacturing company which had been supplying the army with boots, and which now, with the peace, was turning part of its machinery to making civilian shoes and handbags. They were of good design and good quality, meant for the North American export market.

The owner and manager, David Jenkins, was aware that some of his goods found other destinations. Shoes and even handbags which had some slight defect did not get sent abroad but could be sold in the home market as export rejects. Their sale was legitimate, but some perfect models also, mysteriously, became second-class material and were offered for sale in London.

He did not push his goods that way himself but he felt a sympathy when they went thus into the starved home market. What he did draw the line at was the way in which shoes and handbags packed and despatched for export disappeared on the way to America. His insurers did not like it.

He suspected they disappeared at the docks, where there was no doubt pilfering; there was everywhere else.

He imagined that the stolen good were then sold off barrows in street-markets, or out of suitcases in public houses. Or just quietly passed from friend to friend.

The police had it in hand. In the end they would find out who was responsible and where the thefts were made.

He studied his bills of lading: the goods went through the Surrey Docks.

THE MURDERER LEFT the café and continued on the walk to the docks. His working life, although not unstructured, allowed him a kind of freedom.

He did not stand out around the docks, where work hours varied according to the tides. Men came and went at all hours.

Ahead of him stretched the Surrey Docks, that great complex of docks, warehouses, and wharves. Beyond that spun the curve of the river which the docks fed. It was a great stretch of land, hardly ever silent, yet with strangely quiet, deserted nooks.

The entrance to the gates was guarded by police-men who might or might not stop you if they did not know your face. The murderer had no intention of trying them out.

He had an idea of his way. There was a strong Rus-sian influence in the street names here: a short walk down Riga Street, then a left turn into Czar Street and you emerged by a passage between two warehouses which led to Convoy Wharf.

At the right time of day, say at night, when the moon was down, no one need see you take this walk. A moon of course was more romantic if you had to consider a girl's feelings. He might not bother with feelings.

He turned back towards the main road, this time taking a short cut down a little alley which would have appealed to Jack the Ripper. Conduit Court, it was called. He might have gone for Conduit Court him-self, since the buildings that made it up were blind, but he had a need of the river. It never occurred to him that he was in the line of succession to some great murderers. He was himself, alone, as ever.

Ahead of him walked two lightermen. No mistak-ing their individual walk, not quite a sailor's roll, but a tilt to one side, corrected as they walked by a tilt to the other. Both men moved in unison. All who worked on water learn to adjust their walk to the water's movement.

He walked behind, setting his feet down hard. He had no idea that John Coffin was already listening for his tread.

SIX

THE NECK OF THE MURDERER

WHAT DIFFERENCE DID the shoe make? After all his hunting, all his triumph of discovery, nothing much seemed to follow the discovery of the shoe.

John Coffin handed it over and saw no more of it.

Things were going on as a result, no doubt, efforts were being made to trace the provenance of the shoe, but no one told him with what result.

Inside himself he nourished the conviction that he, of all the people interesting themselves in the case, was the most aware of the truth. Hard to know why, since in many ways he was pushed to the side by the men from the Yard, was young and junior in any case. Perhaps it was that as he trudged around Greenwich Wick and Greenwich Hythe he felt untuitively closer to the girl and how she had lived, hence to her killing.

Because in her living was death, no doubt of that.

But his intuition was no logic, it was more like a woody outgrowth to his own character.

Several days passed without much action in them, or not much anyone told him about. He did hear, through the usual channels, that the tiny hand found had been identified as that of an adult chimpanzee, probably from the bombed-out pet shop and private zoo in Greenwich Hythe. The search for the Shepherd child ground to a halt. Tom Banbury had a day off sick, then returned to work.

On the third evening, not having seen Chris or Alex or even Mrs Lorimer ('Mr Coffin, your ration-book, *please*?'), and with the unfair sense of having been abandoned by all, he washed and changed.

He was going to see Stella Pinero. It was his turn. He had stayed away to give Alex and Chris their turn, which was vanity on his part since he had no reason to believe that Stella preferred him to them. So deep inside himself there had to be another reason, which was probably cowardice. You could fear Stella for what she could do to you.

He bought her some roses at the florist's in the arcade near the theatre. He was the last customer, surprised to find it still open.

Unusual, the florist told him, he was lucky, but there had been a large order to work on.

'A wedding?' Coffin asked.

'No. A funeral. Local butcher's widow. Lovely lady.'

'Large family, I suppose?' Coffin could see the huge pile of wreaths grouped at the back of the shop. One spelt her name in carnations, Alice, it said in red and white.

'Lots of friends. Don't think they had any children. Believe they adopted one.'

One wreath was in the form of two initials side by side.

A.C., it said.

Clarke? Clarke, family butcher?

'STELLA?' He knocked on her dressing-room door, the bunch of flowers in his hand, and a buttonhole. 'I'm a stage door Johnnie come to call.'

Stella Pinero had cleaned her face of make-up and brushed her hair, but she still wore her wrapper, with her street dress swinging on the hanger by her side. It was a new dress, underneath were a pair of new white shoes. She had a matching shoulder-bag hanging in the cupboard beside her. Her little secret as yet.

'Come in. Oh, it's you. What do you want?'

'You. Come out to a meal. I didn't think I'd even find you here. Why aren't you at a first-night party?'

'It's *not* the first night, that was last night. It's the second. And a matinée as well.'

'I am sorry, Stella. I truly forgot. It's the way the work has been. Heavy.'

'There *is* a party, as a matter of fact, in someone's dressing-room. Bluebell's, I think. And Eddie's gone to one in London. I could have gone. But I didn't fancy it.'

She was smelling the flowers, early roses. More expensive than they should have been. 'Come out and have a meal with me. The Padovanis'.'

She was tempted, he was easy company, and she needed the uplift. 'We'll go dutch.'

'Sure.' He liked the way actresses always paid their way.

'We could look in on Bluebell's party.'

'I'd like it.' Bluebell was a favourite of his.

'You are nice.' She sighed.

'And you're in a rotten mood.'

'Not arf.' She sighed and held up a mirror to her face. 'It's Candida. Doesn't suit me. And I don't understand her. Rachel says, don't worry, play the part and let the audience do the understanding, but I like to *know*.'

They were alike. He wanted to know also, and in common with Stella he felt frustration. But unlike Stella, he couldn't show it with tears, nor was anyone going to console him with roses.

'Cheer up.'

'I was lousy as Candida, and you know it, that's why you pretended about the first night. And what's more you knew I'd be lousy.'

'No, Stella, that's not exactly true. I could not know that. I'm not telepathic.'

But he had known; he had an insight into Stella Pinero, sometimes sharper than he deserved. He sensed she had a love-affair going with someone, but he didn't know with whom. There were several candidates, and gossip was ready with names. Edward Kelly was one; Chris another. For all he knew he was on the gossip's list himself.

'Don't mind too much.'

'I mind failure.' It had only been comparative failure, the audience had liked her Candida, the gallery would always respond to her star quality, but Stella Pinero judged herself. Also, her peers judged her, and she had known from Eddie's friendly slap on her shoulder as the curtain came down just how far she failed. He was offering her sympathy, damn him. Her relationship with Eddie was not to include sympathy, she would not have it.

Also, the man from the London management had not turned up.

Bluebell appeared at the door. 'Hello, Johnny love, come to my party and bring a girl with you. It's a good party.'

'We'll look in.' Stella was fixing her eyelashes. Little beads of mascara would keep forming and had to be brushed apart.

'You've got that too wet,' appraised Bluebell professionally. 'Why don't you just lick it?'

Stella looked at the block of mascara.

'Because *you* borrowed it and licked it.'

'That's right. I did. I think Bess and Nicky had a go, too.' She frowned. The shortage of Leichner's mascara was a serious worry to her. 'Well, get along. And bring a bottle if you've got one.'

She was gone with a gay little kick of her heels.

'She's in a good mood because she was bloody good as Prossy in *Candida* and she knows it. Also she's going to be a Thames Water Spirit in the Masque and wear a very romantic costume.' Stella's own costume was hideous, but would have to be borne as money was short. Very short.

'Pretty shoes she's wearing.' He had noticed Bluebell's shoes: they were high-heeled and delicate, their colour a pale tan. They did not resemble the shoe he had found in the river but they were pretty and new. The red shoe had been new when Lorna Beezley had gone for her last walk. Coffin did not connect Blue-bell's shoes with Lorna's, but he was a policeman and so he noticed them.

'Yes.' Stella was noncommittal. If he had known her better he would have listened to that note in her voice. As it was, he did notice it (the policeman again) but thought it was envy.

She did not ask him about his own work, she could tell he was tired and jumpy. Instead she said: 'Thanks for looking after me the other night. You were gentle and kind. I don't meet that so often.'

'How did Mrs Esthart take it?'

'How do you expect? She was angry. Inspector Banbury came up to see her, but she sent him away.'

'He wouldn't like that.'

'I wasn't there, but Florrie said he was disappointed. They seem to know each other.'

'I wonder why she did that?'

'I don't know. The bird had a good effect on her, though. Woke her up from her dream world.'

She was waking anyway, Coffin thought, and he found that an interesting process.

'I think she's planning something.'

'Such as what?'

'Such as I don't know. What Rachel doesn't want you to know you don't learn. Even Florrie can't read her all the time, and think of the years she's known her. I'm better in some ways because of being an actress.'

Stella disappeared behind a screen, soon to reappear wearing a dark blue printed silk dress with white shoes. Under her arm she had tucked a white hand-bag.

She had a quick spray of Arpège. In the end Blue-bell had not wanted it: she didn't like the smell, and a more complicated barter arrangement had been entered into involving ten clothing coupons, a pair of nylon stockings, and two copies of American *Vogue*.

'Let's go to the party. Just look in. She's a good kid.'

'Is she really called Bluebell?'

'Christened it, so she says.'

'Something's worrying you, isn't it? And not just Candida.'

'Oh, let's talk about it later, darling. Now let's be bright, gay and the life of Bluebell's party.'

Her Coward imitations were not the best thing she did, which was an intimation that she was of the 'new' style and, within it, was going to be a great classical actress.

AT DINNER, after agreeing to split the bill down the middle, they ordered the Padovani spaghetti and a bottle of the 'special' red wine. Special in that it was marginally more intoxicating than the others. Perhaps it went to Stella's head a little.

Elbows on the table, Stella told him all her hopes and plans. Poured them all out. Pale she might be beneath her rouge, and tired after a strenuous week of performance and rehearsals (*Candida* in repertory now, *As You Like It* in rehearsal, and the Masque being prepared) but underneath energy bubbled.

She started to tell him all her plans and hopes for the future. She was very ambitious. Love, marriage, children, yes, all very well. But for her, work had to come first. She wanted to play Ophelia while still young, Juliet within the next few years if she could, and Hedda Gabler when she was thirty. A few star parts in long runs would not come amiss, but she didn't want to get trapped into the commercial theatre.

He knew all the stories about how ruthlessly Rachel made Stella work at her parts on the small stage she had created in the old stables of Angel House. The tales that Stella sat talking to Rachel Esthart as long as that lady desired, all night if such was her mood, all this he knew, too. He had heard how Stella massaged Rachel's lovely hands keeping them supple, how she brushed her hair and ironed her silk underclothes.

Slavery, some called it. 'Letting Rachel Esthart boss you around,' Bluebell had said, but then she was envious. 'For God's sake don't let her use you, because she will.' Coffin had heard Edward Kelly say that himself.

The fiercest critic was Chris, who was probably the most in love with Stella of them all, and the one to whom she seemed to pay least heed. Occasionally Coffin had noticed Stella gave Chris a kind of measuring look: he wondered what she was measuring him against. Or for.

He admired Stella, loved her even, and almost against his will, but he thought Stella knew what she wanted and what Stella was in the world for.

'Anyway, we got paid this week. Albie and Joan are having a hard time, did you know that? Yes, of course you did, I think everyone does. But *Candida* will fill their coffers even if I am lousy in it.'

Coffin put his hand over hers. 'Cheer up.'

'Just as well the London management man didn't show,' said Stella, pursuing her grievances.

So that was what was worrying her. Coffin put up a hand to the waitress. 'Let's have some more wine.'

Shirley came hurrying over. She loved to serve Stella, the actress she most admired at the moment. As beautiful as Gladys Cooper, as glamorous as Gertie Lawrence, and younger than Shirley was herself. More or less consciously, Shirley was modelling herself on Stella, imitating her style and way of speech.

Thus, by a kind of remote control she was also copying Rachel Esthart whose influence on Stella was already marked.

Those with eyes to see could see these parallel cases.

Coffin did see, with amusement, but not right through Shirley's innocent mirror to Rachel Esthart.

The murderer was one who saw.

Shirley swung off, her full skirt floating upwards as she moved, revealing a flash of sturdy thighs.

Vic Padovani brought the wine to their table himself. 'You'll prefer this wine to the one you ordered.'

Coffin looked at the label. 'More expensive.'

'Have it on the house!' Vic scratched his neck as if he was embarrassed, fidgeting with his collar.

'You sure, Vic?' He knew Vic was bullied by his father, adored by his mother, and persecuted by his sisters.

'The old man's left me in charge.'

'Stay and have a drink with us.'

'No. I'm doing the cooking. I'm needed in the kitchen. We're busy tonight.'

He moved away. Coffin's gaze followed him. He wished he knew how things stood there.

'Do you think we ought to let him give us this?'

'No. But we had to.' There were things you could not say to a man. It was a question of his pride, of which bullied Vic had plenty as Coffin very well knew. But you couldn't expect Stella to understand.

She did, though. In her own way, slanted towards Stella. 'It's like me with Rachel. I know some people think I'm a kind of parasite on her; others think she's blood-sucking me. Not true. I've taken a lot from her, but I've got a lot back. And what I've done I've been proud to do.'

It wasn't quite Vic's position, not the way Coffin, and Vic too, probably, saw it.

'And what about Rachel? How does she feel about it?' He was pushing her, wanted to see what she'd say.

'She knows what I've done for her. She started to come back to life, proper, everyday life as soon as I came. I think that's why Joan and Albie sent me there.'

'I thought it was Eddie Kelly who suggested it.'

'Joan meant it to happen. She's quite a string-puller is Joanie. She saw it was time for Rachel to stop being the sleeping princess.' Stella started another sentence, then checked herself. She wanted to say that she was frightened, her friends were frightened, that the women of Greenwich *knew* there was going to be another victim, and perhaps another. They sensed it.

She poured some wine. 'We're never going to finish all this bottle.'

A group from Bluebell's party surged into the restaurant. Alex Rowley was there, wearing a cheerful grin and talking to Bluebell, who was giggling.

He came over to John Coffin. 'And what are you up to?'

'And what are you?' He looked at Bluebell.

'Drowning my sorrows.'

'Sorrows? You?' said Stella.

'The two men looked at each other. It had been a bad few days. The relationship between them, instead of prospering, had become drier, harder, with each of them looking at the other with doubt.

I'm a good detective, thought Coffin. What's he? I wish I knew.

I notice things about people he doesn't, was the burden of Alex Rowley's thoughts. See more, feel more. I'm a genius, I am. He did smile to himself at that.

'What are you laughing at?' asked Coffin.

'Myself,' said Alex. I don't think he even likes me, he added to himself.

Stella saw Bluebell give a wave and disappear. She got up. 'I'm going to powder my nose.'

The two girls met in the cloakroom. Stella said: 'You were super as Prossy.'

'Thanks.' There was a moment's pause while each girl perfected her lipstick. Then Bluebell looked down at her stocking. She smoothed an invisible wrinkle. Then she turned her head to study the seams. 'Am I straight?'

'Perfect.'

They looked down at their shoes, bright, pretty and new.

'Where did you get those shoes?' asked Bluebell.

Then they both giggled.

As they walked to the door she said: 'So Vic came through?'

'He did.'

'What did you have to do to get them?'

'Nothing much. Just go out a few times with him and let him hold my hand.'

'Is that all?'

'Seems to be all he wants.'

At the door Bluebell said: 'If you weren't at the very top of your form as Candida, it's just because you're a very special kind of actress.'

'You are a nice girl,' said Stella, grateful.

The two of them left together, Bluebell going across to talk to friends and Stella returning to the table with John Coffin.

JOHN COFFIN and Alex Rowley were sitting talking over the wine, heads down, deep in discussion.

Stella looked at them, and decided. Two policemen talking together, that was right, normal, safe. She'd talk; she had something to say.

If she could get through to them. They both seemed deep in their own obsession: John Coffin could think of little but the dead girl from the river, while Alex, like his boss Tom Banbury, was absorbed with the missing Shepherd girl.

'Boys,' she said. 'Listen.' They did not. Their conversation continued.

'Policemen talk, I suppose,' said Stella. 'One degree worse than man's talk.' She sounded aggressive.

'No worse than theatre talk,' said Coffin, giving her his attention. 'If we seem hard to know, theatre folk are even harder, Stella. I never know how to take you. Sometimes you're lovely about each other and sometimes so cruel.'

'We're none of us quite what we seem,' said Stella sadly. 'Not even our names are our own. I'm not called Pinero, Eddie Kelly isn't Kelly, and even Chris took his father's professional name instead of Brown.'

'Come to that,' said Alex, 'I took my step-father's name.'

'Why did you do that?'

'He wanted it.' He added, 'And there was a kind of connection in our names. That made it easier.'

'And I bet you were a Boy Scout too,' said Stella admiringly, 'and had a sheath-knife. In fact, I bet you've still got it.'

'He has,' said Coffin. 'I've seen it.'

'Shut up, you two.' Across the room he had seen Bluebell; he gave her a little wave.

Bluebell sat down in the fourth chair. 'I'm hungry. I want to eat.'

Bluebell was always hungry, happy or miserable, tired or full of energy, end of day or early morning, she was perpetually hungry. She was a dancer as well as an actress so there was a reason behind it. When she stopped dancing she was going to put on weight. It was the dancing that drew her and Alex together.

A crowd had come in from a local cinema, and suddenly The Padovani was crowded, with Shirley and Vic hurrying back and forth with trays. The Padovani was the only eating-place in the district that always seemed able to produce plenty of good food. So it had a large clientele, more than it could always hold. A queue was not unknown at The Padovani, especially at weekends.

'Vic,' called Bluebell. 'Spaghetti, please.'

'You're going to be a fat old lady.'

'I'm going to be a fat old lady,' agreed Bluebell. 'And perhaps even a fat young one, but not with rationing. I never get enough to eat.'

'I'll give you my sweet coupons if you give me...' Stella paused to think. What did she want?

'What have I got that you could possibly want?'

'At the moment, the best notices, but you can't trade those.'

'I'm right out of Tampax.' It was incredible the necessities of life that were suddenly not there.

Bluebell lowered her head. 'Can you tell me where to get some?'

As the girls whispered, Alex said to John Coffin, 'Tom Banbury's sick with himself that he can't find the Shepherd child's body.'

'You don't even know she's dead.'

'Tom's made out she is. She has to be. Where is she, if she's not dead?'

'He's convinced you.' It was a statement, not a question. For himself, he was not so sure. 'I can think of other possibilities. She does not have to be dead at all. Just lost.'

He was looking for someone himself and not doing very well at it.

'A lost child would leave a trace as she moved. She's got to eat. Sleep. Survive. She's only a kid, remember, not a sort of free-ranging pirate. Alone, she's going to show up.'

'Then she will show. Give her time.'

Hang on to that thought; that it took time. It might help with his own search for his sibling.

'Does Banbury tell you everything?'

Without pleasure, Alex said, 'Not by a long chalk. A close bugger. Except with Dander. Talks to him all right. Plenty of talking there.'

'What do you make of Dander?'

'Not much. And I don't think he likes *me* much. Looks at me as if he was measuring me for the drop.'

'Oh, he does that to all of us.'

'He pushed Banbury the way of the Shepherd case, you know. He had the say-so about the Yard and the Beezley death. He could have all of us as a team on it.'

It was the confident voice of the canteen speaking; Alex had picked up the gossip there.

'On to the Shepherd case and off the Beezley murder.' Alex adjusted his tie.

'Same thing.'

'Tom Banbury *wanted* the Shepherd case and Dander knew it. He's got a thing about kids. Lost his own in the Blitz.' So he'd heard: canteen gossip again.

'Warwick doesn't seem a bad chap.' Coffin didn't see much of him, just occasionally, like Caesar with his cohorts, he was seen flashing past. Orders and directives there were, of personal contact little. Warwick *had* his clansmen, but they were old associates, people he'd worked with before, or chaps he brought with him from the Yard. John Coffin was not one of these.

Still, he was grateful for the occasional comment: he got that now and again; the passing word thrown to him.

Like when he'd brought in the shoe.

On the other hand, sometimes he felt in quarantine.

'Banbury ought to go by the evidence.'

'He's got a bit of evidence.'

'Like the hand?'

'No.' Alex dropped his voice. The girls were talking. One thing about actresses, they never lacked for conversation. 'A piece of clothing. A dress. It's been identified as hers.'

'May not mean much.'

'It means something.'

A dress, a shoe, human artefacts pointed to the life or death of two different people. He believed the shoe was important, the dress might be.

'What about you? Anything interesting?' asked Alex.

'Nothing special.' He told Alex about the shoe, waiting to see how he reacted. There was no reaction. Alex thought about it, but apparently did not consider the discovery significant.

'Have they got anything hard?'

Coffin shrugged. 'Clutching at strands, I'd say. Still looking for a likely man, from her friends and lovers. Feeling is he was probably someone she knew.'

Lorna Beezley might only have known her killer slightly, he reflected, but enough to trust him.

'He must be an attractive customer because she goes off with him into the night without a murmur. He's got some neck.'

And by his neck he would hang when found, tried and condemned.

The hanging drop would be assessed according to his weight and height.

'As far as is known.'

'No one's come forward to say they heard a struggle.'

'At night—would they hear? From the river to the road is quite a stretch. Not many houses near.'

None in fact, but there might have been someone passing. London never slept.

'It could be she didn't hear her killer, that he just grabbed her.'

But that was a difficult picture to put together in Coffin's opinion, because in a public place a struggle would have been witnessed. He did not believe, no one in the team on the case believed, that she had gone for a moonlight walk at a time of springtide all on her own. Girls didn't do it.

No, Lorna had known her killer and trusted him. So they were not looking just for a face in a crowd.

'I will say this for Warwick,' he said to Alex, 'he has no sacred cows. He's put every man that Lorna could have had contact with through the machine. Her school, the theatre, this place here—' he motioned to The Padovani—'even to the old chap with the cab at the station and the caretaker at the school. All checked.'

In addition to the soldiers at the nearby Woolwich Barracks and all the lightermen and watermen and dockers. Likewise the crews of docked ships. A big job.

'And no leads?'

'Or none he's admitting to.'

There was a sound of loud voices from the kitchen as Shirley and then Vic emerged as if they had been quarrelling.

'That Vic.' Shirley shook herself like a dog shaking off water. A vivid expression of her feeling.

'Get your coat on and go.' Vic was giving the orders.

'What is it, Shirley?' There had always been a certain chumminess between her women customers like Stella and Bluebell and Shirley, possibly they felt sorry for her, seeing more than the men.

'I got to go home.' She was buttoning her coat. 'And Vic's nagging. I've got to go home and look after the kids, Dad's on night shift and doesn't like them left.'

'And Vic doesn't want you to go?' Stella gave Vic an indignant look.

John and Alex sat back to this, openly listening.

Vic growled something in Italian.

'Damn no,' said Shirley. 'He *wants* me to go. I have to go, there's the kids. I'd rather stay here. They make me sick.'

Vic said, 'You're a bad girl. You should love children.'

'No, she's not.' Stella was indignant. 'She's got a life of her own.'

'Her mother was killed in the Blitz.'

'That's silly talk, Vic.' Shirley's face was red. 'She was not killed in the Blitz; she went off with a Polish soldier while Dad was in North Africa. And Dad wouldn't have her back when he came home. She's not dead. She's living over Wapping way.'

She spoke with all the true-born Londoner's unconscious resentment and scorn for that part of London in which he does not live: Wapping was a nowhere place.

'Meanwhile I'm little mother, damn them. One day I'll cut away and go myself.'

'You do that, Shirley, and you'll be a loose girl.'

'Oh, Vic!' Shirley went to the door, opened it. 'I'm off.' The door banged behind her.

'Shouldn't someone go with her?' asked Stella.

'Girls like Shirley don't come to harm,' said Vic. He was angry.

Stella dropped her voice: 'Vic's upset, so Bluebell says, because he's been questioned about the murder. Well, he would, wouldn't he? Natural. So have Eddie Kelly, and Chris as well. Albie, too, I expect.'

She looked at Coffin in question.

He stared down at the table. Not me. I didn't. I wouldn't enjoy questioning Vic. An old mate.

But for that matter I've been gone over myself, Stella love, although I have not mentioned it. So have Alex and a few other chaps at the station. Six months as detectives, and I'm under suspicion myself for a murder. Not what I expected.

But nothing's come of it.

Zero.

Nix.

Nothing.

He stood up. 'Come on, we'll be off too.' He held Stella's coat for her.

He had picked up the real emotion in that quarrel between Shirley and Vic. People working together do get angry with each other. Shirley was an attractive girl, that probably made it worse.

As they walked into the street there was a glimpse of Shirley cycling away down the hill.

'Where does she live?'

'Somewhere down at Greenwich Hythe. Near the river. Bit slummy.'

Angel House loomed ahead, dignified and sombre in the summer night. There was a rising moon.

'There's something I was trying to get out this evening but couldn't.'

He put his arm around her and they walked up and down outside Angel House. The praying angel seemed to offer them his best wishes, one eye, seen in profile, seeming to look their way.

'It's about Rachel Esthart and the murder?' Only Rachel brought that look to Stella's face. He knew she never put it on for *him*.

'Yes.' Stella started to talk, slowly at first, then with more confidence. 'I've said she is coming out of her withdrawal from the world stage. It started, as I've said, when I went to her. Either it had already begun or she was ready for it anyway. She was coming back into the world after her time out.' Stella added thoughtfully: 'But you don't come out of a thing like that unscathed. Well, do you?'

'No, I suppose not.'

One light was flicked on in Angel House. Probably Florrie's room, high up under the eaves. He watched it. Lovely to have no blackout, no sirens, no bombs. There were a lot of things wrong in his world, but the war was over, he was full of hope. Without realizing it, he pressed closer to Stella.

'Oh, love,' she said. 'Listen. Supposing her mind was affected. Bent. She's an actress beyond anything else. She likes a dramatic moment.'

'So? What are you suggesting?'

'The letter: I wonder if she sent it to herself. There was something very theatrical about it. Artificial, almost.' Stella's voice faltered. 'Also about her performance. That was an act, I swear.' She looked at Coffin for reassurance. 'I feel so disloyal saying this. I love the woman.'

'No, you're right to speak.' He took command. 'Let's go on walking. We must have this out.'

They paced up and down the narrow pavement between the two lamp posts that marked the boundary of the Angel House garden wall. A small summerhouse with a gilded roof marked one corner.

'You're right, Stella, there was—is—something contrived and wrong about that letter. I felt that myself without knowing why. I still don't know why, and I still feel it. You're a good girl, Stella. So you'll tell me the truth.'

'Yes. You know I will.'

'Why do you think Rachel Esthart wrote the card herself?'

'She had a packet of similar cards. They were on her desk. She was looking at them. She saw me, too.'

'What did she do?'

'Nothing. Just put the cards back in a drawer, and went away.'

'That doesn't sound like guilt. There had to be something else.'

'It's just her. She's changed. I'm frightened a bit. John—she couldn't have killed the girl herself?'

'She'd have to be very mad to do that.'

'Has she been so very sane this last fifteen years? I wonder sometimes.'

'Anything else?'

Stella shook her head. 'Except I think Florrie's frightened. She's very jumpy. And nicer to me than usual. She doesn't like me, you know.'

Coffin turned them back towards Angel House. 'No, Stella. It's man crime. All the marks.'

Except there had been no sexual violation. Only mutilation. And hadn't someone once thought that Jack the Ripper was Jill the Ripper?

They were outside Angel House, she had to go in. He hoped to God she was safe. He bent to kiss her.

'I don't suppose you could ever, well, care for me—seriously, I mean?' He felt clumsy, stupid, but the feeling was real.

'I don't know.' She gave a bitter little laugh. 'I'm the classic can't-make-up-her-mind girl. I don't know what I want.'

'Is there someone else?'

'Yes.' She dropped her voice so that he could hardly hear the murmur. 'Sort of.'

More than one, probably. Being Stella, it was probably more than one, and always would be. Yet she knew the part, the career, the way of life she wanted. That was Stella.

'Forget I spoke, love. No harm done.'

She raised her head. Florrie from her window saw their kiss. Rachel Esthart saw them. As their lips met, Stella said: 'I swear she's planning something, Rachel is.'

'You've trusted me with this.'

'I wouldn't have told anyone else. I might have done in front of Alex. No one else.'

'Leave it here. With me. Don't say anything to anyone.'

'I won't.'

Stella went inside.

It might well be she would be safer there than anywhere else.

Coffin had his own dark thoughts which that evening had reinforced.

Dark, dark, like a shadow of comradeship gone wrong.

SEVEN

THE NECK FEELS THE ROPE

THE TINY WOMAN who crouched in the recess between two stone pillars on the wharfside at the Isle of
Dogs did not know she was being talked about by her
sister and her sister-in-law. She was on bad terms with
them both. She was cleverer, prettier and better educated than either of them; they resented her. For her
part she had never liked either of them, nor did she
like water, the Isle of Dogs, or crouching. Life plays
you some nasty tricks.

A little way up river from Greenwich, towards
Deptford, two women were talking.

'Coffee or tea?'

'Tea, please. She's left him, you know. That's what
she's done.'

'Never. She's a wanderer. I see her going off, having an affair, but not leaving him.'

'He says so.'

'He would. It's what he hopes.'

'Oh, go on, Lou.'

They were talking in the small dark living-room of
a small terrace house. It was a house which had been
bombed, then roughly repaired, and was now undergoing re-painting and re-papering. The living-room

was half done. Two walls had new paper in a bright colour while the other two retained the original grubby yellow.

In the kitchen outside a kettle was boiling.

The woman who had offered the choice of tea or coffee looked round nervously. 'I don't like making tea in her kitchen without her being here.'

'Wait long enough if you waited for *her*. Never offered a cup, she didn't, even if she'd got the kettle on herself.' The speaker looked around appraisingly. 'You've tidied up.'

'Did it for him, didn't I? He's had enough to put up with.'

'Any sugar, Lou?'

'Oh, ought we to use their sugar? I never like touching another person's rations.'

Lou occasionally annoyed everyone. At the moment she was annoying her friend, Nora, who was sister to Jim who was married to Lou's own sister Eileen, always called Tiny because of her size. The chain of relationships did not end there because Lou was married to Ted, who had once been engaged to Nora before she married Arthur on the rebound from a quarrel with Ted. Nor was that the end of it because Eileen and Jim had one child who was at present being passed back and forth between them like a parcel. He was unfortunate enough to resemble his pretty mother while bearing the sex of his father, thus endearing himself to neither aunt. Lou could not 'abide' boys, while Nora disliked Eileen's looks. She liked boys, though, and was possibly the little chap's best hope at the moment.

A wail from his pram outside alerted the aunts. Lou went outside and wheeled in the pram.

'Fancy leaving your child.' Even a boy deserved something better, but Eileen never thought twice about anyone else.

'Fancy leaving your husband like that! And him just back from active service.' Nora picked up the boy, a child of some eighteen months and gave him a biscuit. 'There you are, Lennie, you take the nice biccy. You'll stop looking such a nancy boy when you get older. She ought to stop putting him in a dress, Lou. It's not right.'

'She didn't take her clothes. Nor her suitcase,' said Lou uneasily. 'Jim said. He doesn't like it.'

'We don't know that for sure. She's been buying a lot new lately. Had more than Jim. Took all his coupons.'

'Mine too,' Lou said sadly. 'Said she'd pay me back. Never has. But she'll be back. She'd never leave Jim really. Just go off for a change. She said so in her note: "Look after baby while I'm out. Back soon, love, Tiny." That doesn't sound like leaving him. Not for ever.'

'So what's Jim done?'

Nora no longer lived close: she had been bombed out, and moved a bus ride away to New Cross. She'd been bombed there too, but less thoroughly.

'Not much. What can you do?'

'He's had over two weeks. I'd have got track of her by now. Look for the man. She's gone off with a man. She's a loose woman.'

'She's not loose,' defended her sister sadly. 'But she does like a bit of fun.'

On the table between them was yesterday's evening paper, which had the latest report on the case of the dead girl found at Greenwich.

Lou picked it up, studying idly while she drank her tea. It was a pity when girls got themselves murdered, but they had only themselves to blame.

THE WOMAN who crouched in the hiding-place stirred uneasily, waiting for the moment to make her re-entrance.

'Stay there,' her boyfriend had said, 'and I'll come and get you, Tiny. Promise.'

He spoke in the way people sometimes talk to children and animals. Toy-talk, paper thin. Such talkers are not usually very fond of either children or animals.

He put his hand to his neck as if it irritated him. There was a red mark where possibly his collar had rubbed, producing perhaps a touch of eczema. The line of red was about two inches long and half an inch wide. There was a wheal-like quality to it as in a rope-burn; the hangman's mark.

EIGHT

THE HANDS OF THE MURDERER

IT DID NOT TAKE LONG to find out something of what Rachel Esthart was planning because she announced it herself, sending out invitations.

Time had passed. Stella endured her role in *Candida*; felt she was improving without enjoying it much, went for an interview with the management in the West End (Lonsdale's, it was, as it happens) where the impresario patted her hand and said: 'You're true gold, darling, but we must wait for the right thing to come along or we shall waste you.' Then he asked her to lunch at the Dorchester and then to see his collection of theatrical relics, but Eddie had warned her about that, as indeed had Bluebell, Joan and Florrie, but not Rachel who had smiled enigmatically, so she said yes to the lunch and no to the playbills and Mrs Siddons's slippers. The lunch was delicious and she could live on that for a week.

Preparations for the Masque gathered pace. The timetable for the Royal Visit progressed through the borough. Special police arrived to check on details. Two Doggett Coat and Badge-winners, both watermen resident in Greenwich, came to blows over which should row the Royal Barge. Then it was announced

there was not to be a Royal Barge, the royal party
would arrive and depart in Daimlers. The watermen
joined in drinks at the Admiral's Head to deplore this
sad dropping away from standards.

'The old Queen would have ridden on the river,'
said the one.

'She's been gone since the turn of the century.'

'I don't mean Victoria: Elizabeth. You remember
her from history.'

Elizabeth and Great Harry her father, Czar Peter
and his reluctant host John Evelyn, were still figures
that walked in Greenwich. There was one family of tall
giant men that called themselves Peters and claimed
descent from Peter the Great. One of them now was
fighting to play a part in the Masque. A claim resisted
strongly by Joan and Albie and promoted by the local newspaper: the *Greenwich Herald*. In the interests
of publicity the current Peter was likely to win.

By now anxieties about the murder were rampant in
Greenwich. The Wick and the Hythe were downright
nervous. Women locked their doors, did not go out at
night alone. It was worse than the blackout, more
nerve-racking than the Blitz. Dark rumours floated in
the air like droplets of the plague. Another girl had
been murdered, only her body had not yet been discovered, or the police were keeping quiet about a series of sex attacks, that was another story.

At Lorimer's both Alex and John Coffin were
questioned and returned tactful answers.

No, no other body. No, no reports of sexual attacks on girls or women. Yes, they were quite sure the

murderer of Connie Shepherd had been caught. They'd got the right man who would very soon be coming up for trial. Yes, her daughter was still missing, but they had no reason to believe she was dead.

No reason to believe anything one way or another about that child. She could be on the moon, for all they knew.

The clothes found had certainly been hers once, but a neighbour had given witness that she had long outgrown them and they had been passed on to her own child (coupons, you know) before being discarded as outworn.

Her own child was there, alive, and kicking its heels while it looked at Tom Banbury and Alex Rowley. Banbury need not have been there, Alex could have done this interview on his own, but Banbury was here, there and everywhere these days, and never seemed to leave him alone.

Some days after his supper with Stella, when a lull, a lassitude, had fallen on the investigation, John Coffin sat at an early breakfast at Mrs Lorimer's. She had a kipper for him, cooked with bacon, a bonus for a good boy. She was getting to like him.

She had a packet of letters the postman had just delivered in one hand and a teapot in the other. 'Tea?'

'Thanks.' The kipper was good, the bacon even better. The day was beginning well. He cast his eye on the letters. Probably none for him, there never were any for him. He had no one to write to him. Never had had. He wondered how it would be to have a wife to write to him.

One could not imagine Stella writing to him, somehow, but that undiscovered brother or sister might if ever located.

Mrs Lorimer poured herself a cup of tea. She never ate with her lodgers, but often attended their meals rather in the manner of a keeper at the zoo, sometimes allowing herself a drink, as now.

There was something in her determined manner of sipping the tea that suggested to him that she wanted to talk.

'Of course, I tell them it is nonsense to suppose the Royal Visit will be put off on account of one murder,' said Mrs Lorimer. 'The King and Queen did not leave London during the bombs so one murder will not drive them away. As a magistrate I can say that with certainty. They *may* leave the princesses at home. One could understand *that* precaution. As a mother of a daughter I would sympathize.'

So the depressed-looking young woman who occasionally emerged from the kitchen was her daughter. Coffin had speculated.

'Are you a magistrate, Mrs Lorimer?'

'I have just become one,' said Mrs Lorimer, with her hanging-judge look on her face.

Lady Olivia's voice could be heard from behind her door. 'Two seemly young men. One so dark and the other that ginger-gold which is so fascinating.' Coffin blushed. 'I choose him.'

One never seemed to see Lady Olivia, although her voice was heard, but she must get around because she was always up to date with the news.

Her door banged to and she began to sing: 'My love is like a red, red rose.'

Of course, she'd seen him go past with the roses for Stella that night, the old devil.

'Don't mind her,' said Mrs Lorimer. 'With gin and whisky so short she's not a lot of trouble. It'll kill her in the end, of course.'

'She'll go down singing.'

Mrs Lorimer laughed for the first time in their aquaintance. 'That she will. But she's an old duck, really. I've known her all my life. My grandmother was cook to her ladyship's mother.'

'Did they live round here?' It struck him that Mrs Lorimer might help him with his own private question. 'I suppose you know a lot of the old family. And the shops?' he continued hopefully.

'No as to Lady Olivia, her family's house overlooked Hyde Park,' said Mrs Lorimer, reverting to the face without a smile, 'but yes, I suppose I know a good many of the local people.'

'I'm interested in Clarke's, the butcher's.'

'There's a whole string of Clarke's all over Greenwich Wick and the Hythe and very good shops they are. Started with one little shop in Greenwich Strand in 1880. Old Mr Clarke's long gone. Be over a hundred now if he were still alive. Always gave good weight. It paid, you know.'

'Ah.'

'We lost touch during the war so I don't know what became of them all. They weren't a large family. I heard the grandson died as a POW in a Jap camp and that *his* wife was dying. But I don't know for sure. The war killed a lot off, one way and another.'

'No family left, then?' Not even one last old man? he thought sadly.

She didn't answer. Instead she put one long, cold hand on his. 'I expect there is a lot you know about this murder that you aren't telling us.'

He realized what he'd done now. She thought he suspected the unlucky family of butchers. Shades of Jack the Ripper.

'It's a private inquiry,' he said hastily. That'd be something; to flush up a long lost brother and then find he was a murderer. He swallowed. I'm laughing, he told himself, just laughing.

'They wouldn't really put off the Royal Visit?'

'I haven't heard a word about it.'

'No.' She considered. 'It was you that got the shoe out of the river. No, don't answer. I know you're not supposed to talk. But I know it was you because Lady Olivia's little friend Paul Shanks, who does her errands for her, was the one who spoke to you. We all wonder you're still alive, taking in that water. Very dirty, you know.'

'I'm all right. I didn't swallow any. But I can't talk about it.'

'That's what Tom Banbury always says. Poor Tom.'

'Well, he's not a talker,' said Coffin with feeling.

'Ah, you didn't know him before his wife went.'

'I thought she was killed.'

'She was killed. By a bomb. With the baby. But she'd gone first. Left home. Moved in with another man. Couldn't stand being married to a policeman. Some women can't.'

'I've heard.'

'Tom feels she wouldn't have been killed if she'd stayed with him. His house was never touched, you know. Not a scratch. And of course, the child that was to be. He minded that. Dug in the rubble with his own hands, he did.'

'Thanks for telling me.'

'Just thought you ought to know.' She added gruffly, 'He'd never tell you himself. He went off to the war after the bomb and did very well, for a bit.'

'I know.' Coffin had done a little prudent questioning himself and knew that Tom Banbury had conducted investigations into refugees from the Low Countries and France who might be Fifth Columnists. If he decided they were spies, then more or less on his say-so they went off to be executed.

What that did to a man in his emotional state could not be guessed at.

'He'd hate killing, poor Tom. But any policeman would, wouldn't he?'

'Yes,' said John Coffin. 'Policemen don't like killing.' But he wondered if that was true: the impulse to kill could come to any man, given the right circumstances. The war taught you that. All you could say was that some men suffered more.

'It was bad about the bird. The seagull.'

'How did you hear about that? Not Lady Olivia again?'

Mrs Lorimer smiled. 'No, the lady who comes in by the day to clean my kitchen scrubs the kitchen floor at Angel House once a week. She told me. Her floor-clothes were all wet and bloodstained. She nearly had a heart attack. It must be connected.' She nodded her head sagely. 'And you really have no idea about the killer?'

'No. Not me. The boss may have.'

'Could it be anyone local?'

He shrugged. 'Could be. Likely in a way.'

A roster of names ran through his mind continually. Edward Kelly, Chris, even Rachel Esthart herself, together with other faces.

'I'll tell you: sometimes I think one thing and sometimes another.'

'Not Rachel Esthart's missing son?'

'I shouldn't think so, would you?'

'No. I'm sure he's dead long since, poor little boy.'

'You knew him?'

'He was only a baby. But he was gentle. Whatever happened, I don't see him as a killer.'

But someone did not like Rachel Esthart, and did not like women. Possibly did not like actresses, but they did not have to be the same person. The killer and the bird man could be two different people.

'There are two aspects,' he said aloud. 'There's the hatred of Rachel Esthart which seems displayed. Then there is the actually killing of the girl, her murder. It's hard to see where the two themes join up. Or why.

'I think that's what worries Dander and Warwick. I know it's what worries me. They play it down. But I think they do join. That I swear.'

It was one point where, he suspected, he parted company with the team from the Yard. He thought he could see the join.

'Mrs Lorimer?'

No harm in talking to Mrs Lorimer, she was as near as nothing to a magistrate, wasn't she?

'You know you're the only person who's mentioned the son as a child. Admitted to knowing him.'

'We all knew him. That was the tragedy. We were on her side. Nicholas Esthart was a bully and a lot else beside. But when they went, when the child disappeared and then was found drowned—well, there was a lot of hostility shown to her. We understood when she withdrew.' With surprising tolerance she said: 'Of course she went too far. That's the theatrical side of Rachel. But she was getting better, cutting down the drink. That is, until she got the card supposed to be from the boy.'

'Must have been a nasty moment. No chance she sent it to herself?'

'Never. If that's what you think, you're mad. It was a shock to her all right. I saw her and I know. I told her to laugh it off, but she couldn't. Well, could you?'

If it was genuine, no.

'I think she's thought it over,' he said carefully, 'and decided it's her way out.'

So in Rachel Esthart's story the card was playing a part the writer of it could not have expected. Why had it seemed a good idea to the murderer to send one card, then to attach another one to the murdered girl?

He wanted to get another look at that card now reposing in the forensic science laboratory across South London. A way would have to be found. If possible without Banbury or Warwick knowing. Or anyone else.

'You saw the dead girl, didn't you.'

He nodded.

'There wasn't a lot of detail in the papers.'

'You wouldn't want to know.'

'Very bad, was it?'

'I think so.'

'Makes you wonder what sort of a person could do a thing like that.'

A man with strong, clumsy, wicked hands, thought Coffin.

Strong because they had strangled the girl.

Clumsy because the buttons on her cardigan had been put on the wrong holes.

Wicked because these hands killed.

A man with a confident stance, a man with an assured walk, a man whose feet stepped out secretly.

He was getting quite a picture of the murderer; he just had to fix on a face.

'That shoe you found, Paul Shanks said it was a very pretty shoe. Red, he said.'

'I wonder he didn't give an interview to the press.'

'He did,' said Mrs Lorimer seriously. 'But his grandmother whacked him and took the money away.'

'He'll go far, that boy.'

'Yes, they do, that family. They're very good at making money. But they can't seem to keep their hands on it.'

Paul was obviously running true to form.

'He's a nice boy. He delivered our papers, you know.' Then she added: 'He would like to speak to you.'

'OK.' Coffin was into his kipper where he had suddenly found a tough area. 'Any time.' He envisaged Paul Shanks dropping in one evening.

'Oh, good.' She opened the dining-room door. 'Come in, Paul.'

He came in, a scruffy, even shabby figure in old blazer and grey shorts. He wore, eccentrically, a Wolf Cub's cap on his head.

He swept it off as he entered the room and put it in his pocket. Carefully, as if it was a treasured object.

Thus quietly does fate introduce a major figure in your life.

Coffin stopped chewing. 'Hello, Paul.'

No answer. There was a deep frown on the boy's face.

He tried again. 'Paul?'

'Mister. Sir—Sergeant.'

'Call me Coffin.'

'You can call me Eagle. I *am* Paul. But my professional name will be Eagle Scott. Or Scott Eagle; I haven't decided yet.'

'Professional?'

'As a detective. I'm going to help you. Get you the news from the street. Stuff you could never get. I have my helpers.'

Coffin thought about it: he too had his fantasies, had had more when he was Paul's age. 'I can't use you publicly. The police don't work like that. You understand?'

'Oh no. A private arrangement.' Then he added hastily, 'No charge; I do it for free.'

'Ah. Good.'

'At first.'

Coffin said, 'Ah,' again. Then he said, 'Thanks Eagle. Or Scott. I'm grateful. I've got to be off now.' He looked around for Mrs Lorimer, who had tactfully withdrawn.

'You think I can't help you. But I can. You'll find out. The shoe you found. Pretty, wasn't it. Won't find shoes like that everywhere. You look in a shoe shop.'

Carefully Coffin said: 'Where will you find them?'

'Ah. I'm working on it.' He paused for effect, then relented. 'Try Woolwich Market.'

Coffin remembered the vegetable stalls, the fish stalls, all grouped in a cluster on one side of the tramway tracks with the cheap clothes stalls and the second-hand bookstalls across the way with trams clanging down the middle. The most proletarian working-class of markets with none of the flashy glamour of Petticoat Lane.

'On a stall?'

'Might be a barrer—or the kerb or a suitcase. Haven't seen, just guessing.'

'You've seen something, or I'm not going.'

'Thought I did. From the top of a tram by the Arsenal.'

Coffin got up to go. 'I might pop down for a look.' He felt in his pocket, slipped a coin into a hand which did not refuse it.

Not a bad idea, he thought, bright boy, but he'd keep it to himself. Information from Eagle Scott was not something you passed on lightly.

And he did have a letter. Mrs Lorimer had left his post in the hall for him to pick up as he passed.

There was only one, a letter with handwritten address. The envelope was square and thick, splendid handmade paper. The writing on it was bold, and noble. He had to say it: noble. The curves were wide, round, the loops gracious. The write of that letter had to be good.

He opened the letter: it was from Rachel Esthart.

In fact, it was not a letter, but an invitation. He was invited to dinner and a 'reception' at Angel House in three days' time.

Not black tie, it said, which was fortunate because Coffin did not have, and so could not have worn, anything except his best demob suit. No thing of beauty in itself, but wearable.

Three days was short notice but he would go. He could see from another envelope on the hall table that Alex had a similar invitation. No doubt there were others in circulation. Would Lady Olivia be there? Stella would be, that was sure. The dinner was on Sunday, there had to be a reason for that.

What was Rachel Esthart up to?

In the sort of crime book he read in his spare time, like Ellery Queen or Anthony Berkeley, there was nearly always a 'confrontation' scene with all suspects present.

In those fictional cases it was usually the detective who arranged it, and the plot was about five pages from its end.

Rachel Esthart's party looked similar. But different, which was what you would expect from life, which so often follows art but never exactly.

Coffin did not put it quite like that; instead, he said to himself, tucking the letter away in a pocket: 'Stella was right then, she *was* planning something.'

A curious fact about the missive worried him.

He pulled the invitation out of his pocket to check what worried him.

Yes, he was quite right. Whether by accident or design, Rachel Esthart had written her invitation to dinner on a card of the same type that the killer had used. But she had omitted the red stain. Or life had.

Down the hill he saw Paul Shanks, alias Eagle Scott, alias Scott Eagle, cycling away, occasionally stopping to push a newspaper through a door, Angel House included. The papers (*The Times* by the look of it, together with the *Daily Mirror* for Florrie) would be late there today. Coffin set out behind him, observing the active figure. He thought:

I gave that boy a coin and a hearing because he reminds me of myself when young. Not that I wanted to be a policeman, I didn't know life had that in store for me, I think I wanted to be a cricketer.

He thought about that boy who had run about the back streets, who had chalked a wicket against an old brick wall and bowled googlies. When he wasn't pretending to be Len Hutton hitting a six over the boundary.

Presumably at about the same time Alex had been trying on his dancing-shoes. Or had he used plimsolls like Coffin, letting imagination do the rest?

Paul Shanks cycled on, still being Eagle Scott, but with the figure of Paul Shanks rising from his back seat to murmur anxiously about being late for school. Eagle pushed him back, but this time he would not go under, he emerged briskly from the underside and reminded Paul there was fried bread for breakfast.

The pair sped off. They passed the murderer, also yoked to his double persona, only not enjoying it so much.

''Morning,' said Paul Shanks, now firmly in the saddle.

The two knew each other, but the murderer did not answer.

COFFIN GOT into the police laboratory to peek at the card found on the dead girl. They were keeping it under specially humid conditions so that it would not dry out. He confirmed his memory of the stain. He asked a question.

The technicians said it was a vegetable stain. They thought he came with Inspector Warwick's knowledge. It *could* be beetroot, they said. They thought it was amusing. There was quite a lot of beetroot wine around in London at the moment, some very nicely bottled with good labels. Also damson wine, and they had heard also carrot.

Coffin took the laboratory worker he knew best out for a drink; he wanted to see if he could get some more specific information on that stain, rather than a joke.

Over a drink his friend offered what he had.

The stain? Vegetable, as he had said earlier, but that was just an informed guess because he had seen other vegetable stains. Experience was what he was offered, and when Coffin pressed for more exactitude he laughed. 'In twenty years' time with better techniques and finer instruments I *might* be able to tell you exactly what ingredients went into the stain. Here and now I can just call it vegetable.'

And Coffin had to remember that the Thames water had soaked it, too, he added. Coffin did remember.

But his friend, over yet another drink, offered the information that scattered over the girl's clothing, still clinging to her in spite of her immersion, were small fragments of brickdust and cement. These were also to be found in and around the points of entry of her wounds, suggesting that knife, and hence the murderer's clothing, had been in contact with a re-building site.

'That's most of London,' observed Coffin. But it was worth thinking about.

Over the next few days he collected a tally of the guests at Rachel Esthart's coming dinner-party. Stella was going to be there, as were Albie and Joan. (Can't really spare the time, darling, ought to be getting on with learning my lines, but can't let Rachel down.) Alex had accepted, and said he'd heard that Chief Superintendent Dander had been asked, but could not confirm this. Certain it was that Edward Kelly and Chris Mackenzie had invitations.

'New friends and old lovers,' was how the Greenroom gossip labelled it. All who were going were envied, all who were not going said they would not have been able to go if asked.

An invitation to Buckingham Palace would have been nothing to it.

Stella, grimly working away at *As You Like It* which was to follow *Candida*, while at the same time rehearsing the Masque in any spare moments, said she had no idea what the party was about, except that the food would be good and Vic was coming in to serve. The Padovani closed on Sundays.

Behind these few days was a background of hard work on what the papers were calling the riverside murder! As reports that might contain a gem of crucial information filtered through they had to be checked over.

Like the woman living in Rodney Row, which ran parallel to the river, who said she had heard a scream on the night in question. There might be something in it, or there might not, but it had to be investigated.

As it turned out, the scream that lady had heard had been her own and led to a rape inquiry. This had been her way of starting the complaint off. Women did sometimes take a circuitous route to a complaint of rape, rather like going to a doctor because of insomnia when what you thought you had was cancer.

Coffin was not responsible for investigating this story, although he heard about it, but he did trudge around calling on the man who wished to confess that he was the murderer, but who had already been placed under sedation by his doctor when Coffin arrived. He did, however, manage to confirm from the man's sister that her brother had been in bed with a high temperature on the night of the murder and quite unable to walk at all.

Coffin also checked shops, flats and houses, asking questions and getting not much in the way of answers. He made careful reports to Inspector Warwick.

At the same time Tom Banbury and Alex Rowley were in Birmingham and Charlton respectively, where sightings of the Shepherd girl had been reported. She was not there. But she was somewhere, because Tom said so and, alive or dead, she had to be. Alex thought they might find her; Coffin thought not. He smelt death. No words passed on the subject: it was possible to convey information like that without comment.

They were aware, both of them, that there was a close liaison between Tom Banbury and Chief Superintendent Dander, and that there was more information around than they were privy to.

At intervals the paths of John Coffin and Alex passed when they looked at each other with question and concern. A scrutiny rather than a friendship.

Coffin longed desperately for friendship. It wasn't coming.

IT WAS A TWO-TRAM RIDE with a change on the way to Woolwich: Coffin surveyed the scene from his chosen seat at the top.

He looked down on the stalls surrounded by crowds, each barrow having its own little cluster of customers, some standing to look, others moving on so that the groups formed and then dispersed. From the top of his tram he could trace one red-coated woman's progress from stall to stall. By the kerb he saw a man crouching over an opened suitcase.

He was happily staring down when he saw a small cycle speeding through the traffic parallel with the tramlines. The coppernob was recognizable at once. Paul Shanks, wearing the persona of Eagle Scott, was speeding to his assistance.

Then his tram moved on, and he got out just around the corner from the Royal Arsenal.

It was late on Saturday afternoon, his first chance to come here.

He walked across the pavement to stare into the window of The Pioneer Bookshop. The window was full of a scholarly-looking book on the history of the working-class: volume one, *The Industrial Proletariat*; volume two, *The Rise of the Union*.

Eagle parked his cycle on the kerb against a lamp post and padlocked it.

'How did you *get* here? How did you know I was coming?'

'Been keeping an eye out. You nearly gave me the slip, though, because you came straight from work.' He grinned. 'But I got word. Had someone on the alert. You need me.'

'If you say so.'

'The man who sells the shoes is here. I saw him.'

'I think I did.' There had been that flash of something interesting at the kerb by the funeral parlour in Powis Street.

'He'll know you're a policeman.'

'I'd thought of that.'

'He'll run.'

'I'd thought of that, too.'

'He'll be gone before you get there. He has men watching. Out-men, they call them. They'll signal as you pass.'

'I expect I'll manage.' He started to walk away.

He took a side path up through the stalls towards where the man with the suitcase had been.

The boy hung back; Coffin felt bad about the brush-off, but it was all for the best.

He passed between two rows of fish stalls, and came up to where the street trader crouched over three suitcases on the opposite pavement. He saw the man clearly. They *were* shoes he was selling. A bus and a horse-drawn dray passed down the road between them.

When he looked again the pavement was clear. 'Damn.' He did see the man, suitcase in hand, departing round the corner of Powis Street, past a jeweller's shop. Behind the man a small figure on roller-skates sped in pursuit.

Eagle was on the job.

He shot ahead of the man, turned back, then deliberately ran into him. They both fell, the suitcase burst open.

From behind two other men and a woman appeared, and closed in on the pair.

Coffin started to run.

He got there in time to lift Eagle to his feet. He had the beginnings of a black eye. The man and his friends, together with the suitcase were disappearing in the crowd.

'Poor kid,' said a woman.

'What good did that do, now?' said Coffin.

Eagle looked up at him and grinned. From beneath his jacket he produced a shoe.

It was twin to the one found in the river.

NEXT DOOR to The Pioneer Bookshop was what had been a milk-bar before the war, when milk was unrationed and cream was to be had. Coffin had almost forgotten what cream was, but one day it would be back, together with ice-cream. He remembered the days of the Wall's Ice-cream man pedalling his little frozen cart. 'Stop me and buy one.' But he had always been an Eldorado man himself.

Eagle had lemonade; he drank coffee, pale and thick with dried milk incorrectly mixed.

Eagle was jubilant. 'I did well, didn't I? Will the shoe help?'

John Coffin placed it on the table in front of him. 'Yes. Probably it will. I can't say for sure.'

'Was he the murderer?'

'No, I don't think so.'

'Will you catch him?'

'The shoe merchant? Yes, probably. And find out where he's getting the shoes.'

Then perhaps fix a connection between the murdered girl and the supplier of black market shoes. And then, in the end, that connection might have nothing to do with her murder.

Even if it led to something, he might never find out himself exactly what part the shoe had played.

Nevertheless he would hand over the shoe and tell the tale. Somewhat edited, of course, not making too much of Eagle's part. Nor could Eagle ever be told very much.

He realized he was treating Eagle Scott just as his own superiors treated him.

'You're a good lad,' he said. 'Bike all right?'

'Sure.'

'And what will you say to your mother about your eye?'

Paul Shanks at once emerged into view, a tired, grubby little boy; Eagle Scott had temporarily retired.

'Don't live with Mum. Mum's dead. I live with Gran. She's all I've got.'

If true, it was something else they had in common. It must have been tough being a child in the war. He said as much. Paul looked surprised (he was all Paul at the moment). 'Oh no, I liked it. Never been anything but war till now. I don't remember anything else.' The child of war added cheerfully: 'I'm off, you coming?'

Coffin looked through the back of the boy's eyes to himself as a boy and saw that they were not the same person after all, their pasts had been different and their futures would be also.

'No. I'm just going to look in at that butcher's across the road. They might have something I want. And *not* meat.'

Paul Shanks cycled off to his home. Coffin crossed the road to William Clarke, Butchers, which was still open.

Ten minutes later Coffin took a tram and then another back to the police station in the old school. In his pocket he had the shoe. The heel was sticking out, pressing against his neighbour in the seat on the crowded tram, so that the man looked at him strangely. Coffin was glad to get off the tram.

Warwick was still at work in the large, bare room which he had made his own. An assistant sat typing away at a table beside him. Warwick was staring into space as if he was thinking.

He received the shoe without enthusiasm.

'Another shoe. You a shoe man?' He took it up, giving it a good hard look. 'Still, it may be useful.'

From him that was praise. Or almost.

'You go off on your own like this much?'

'No, sir.'

'Your idea is that by following it up we make a connection with her murderer?'

'Well, nothing else has.'

'He's one of the men we've talked to. One of the many. But which?' Warwick balanced the shoe on his hand. 'This may help. Thanks.'

Praise at last.

'What are you doing now?'

'I'm off duty, sir.'

'Forget it...' Warwick looked thoughtful. 'It's Saturday. Probably not much doing down in the Surrey Docks, but you can have a try. And here's a list of names and addresses for you. Yes, others besides you have been doing some thinking. There's a man in Birmingham who's been shouting about a consignment of shoes he's lost.'

There went Saturday and unless he was lucky, Sunday and its dinner-party, too. But he felt very cheerful. This was real work.

And in his pocket he had the Christian names, Willy Alfred, of a real live member of the Clarke family butchers. The Clarkes had sold out before the end of the war, but the family went on, war or not. Hope, he thought, that was what carried you forward. In spite of what his landlady had said, a member of the family survived.

NINE

THE WORK OF THE MURDERER'S HANDS

AT THE PADOVANI, they were shouting for Shirley; at the Theatre Royal they were shouting for Stella. Joan Delaney, sitting huddled over her accounts with Albie full of gloom by her side, heard the shouts.

Stella soon shouted back. Yes, what the hell was all the noise about, she was just coming. She appeared, flushed and untidy, according to observers.

Holding up her skirt, she ran to the wings to wait her cue. Albie was very strict about performers being there ready to walk on.

At The Padovani, Shirley did not answer. She had not turned up for work that night, the busiest of the week, Saturday.

If Stella had been missing for an hour everyone would have been out looking for her. At The Padovani, everyone shouted for Shirley, cursing because she was not there to work, but no one went looking.

Coffin dropped in for a sandwich and a drink on his way home. He was tired, telephone talk tired, having been talking to Birmingham. He was also dejected because he had been to the address in Charlton, and a V2 rocket had got it in 1944 and the whole house had gone. The neighbours said other members of the

Clarke family survived elsewhere in Charlton, but they did not know which address. So that was a dead end. Temporarily. There was always hope.

Vic was being abused for not having checked Shirley was here, for being slack, for its being, somehow, his fault.

He was calling out that he didn't know where Shirley was, why should he? She was no girlfriend of his.

'You're up to every girl,' said his sister Nina, pushing past with Coffin's sandwich, to which she had attended personally, she had her eye on him. 'I've seen you.'

'Shut up.' Vic stood at the kitchen door wearing his white apron, and handling his big carving knife like a weapon.

'Victor!'

Vic looked at Coffin in appeal. 'I've been penned in the kitchen all day, how can I be everywhere?' Save me, he was saying to Coffin.

'And last night too, Victor?' Nina put a glass of wine by Coffin's right hand. Nice hands he had, she appreciated that. 'Were you everywhere last night, too?'

'Last night was my night off.'

'Well, we didn't see Shirley, so we assumed...'

'Assumed, assumed. She asked for last night off because her father was ill. I was at the pictures. On my own.'

Vic went into the kitchen, the door swung behind him to be followed by the sound of dishes crashing.

In the matter of dramatic effects the Padovanis needed no teaching from the Theatre Royal.

The next morning Coffin arrived by two trams and one bus, at the Surrey Docks. It was Sunday, but the river never closes down because the tide keeps coming in, and ships must load or unload their cargo according to the passage of the moon as it pulls at the waters. The Thames is a splendidly tidal river which, depending on the season, produces either a spring or a neap tide, the one very high, the other very low.

Coffin knew where to go. He followed a path from the main road, through the main dock gates to the Convoy Walk.

His path had been determined by his conclusions from among his series of telephone calls yesterday about the shoes. Some of the telephone calls had been fruitless, but some had yielded gold.

Consignments of women's fashion shoes, made in Birmingham, and destined for the North American export market (this earned dollars and pleased Sir Stafford Cripps) had been discovered to be short, by several hundreds of pairs, when they came to be loaded.

At exactly which point the carefully packed shoes had been lifted was not clear. The boxes and crates remained, apparently undisturbed, but were empty.

After bitter complaints from the Birmingham manufacturer and his agent in London at the time they were taking, it was established (as Birmingham had claimed all along) that the thefts were taking place on the dockside just before loading.

The local police maintained an office and staff on the dock itself, and this office, working with the Deptford station and the Greenwich one, had arrived at a group of suspects.

They thought they knew the small group of men, all casual labour at the docks, doing the actual thefts. These men were probably aided by the night-watchman.

More important, they thought they could name the man who paid for the thefts to be done, received the shoes when stolen, and then passed them on to the men who would quietly sell them.

It was a small neat operation, as a result of which quite a few feet in South London were going prettily shod.

It was almost entirely a South London affair. Some black-market shoes were to be seen on sale in Oxford Street, a few in Petticoat Lane, but in general this outlet was outside the scope of this small criminal. He didn't want to go big; he knew his limitations. He kept it local.

He was thought to be Joe Leopardo, a second-generation Italian immigrant living at New Cross, South London, above his jeweller's shop.

The lines of the murder case and the black-market investigation had crossed at this point.

The local police did not see Joe Leopardo as a murderer; he was a small, devout man, with a loving wife.

All the same, as Coffin walked on he felt he was closer to what was really going on in the investigation

than he had been before. By luck, and aided by Eagle
Scott, he got himself a perch on the inside circuit.

As a kind of superstitious gesture of respect, he had
bought the current issue of the *Beano* ('The Scott's
Laddie's Highland's Chase') and had it in his raincoat pocket with the *News of the World*.

It was raining slightly. Down river, Stella was preparing to step on to a barge in a rehearsal of the
Masque. She was the Lady arriving on the broad
bosom of the Thames to meet Gloriana. She was getting very wet. At Mrs Lorimer's, a piece of roast beef
of sinewy disposition was being put into the oven for
the lodgers' Sunday lunch.

Coffin thought happily that if he got things here
over quickly he would be back in time for Sunday
lunch, and then, if he was even luckier, he could stand
on the river bank and watch Eddie Kelly make a fool
of himself dancing a fandango to Chris Mackenzie's
music. He knew the evil rhythm that Chris had put
into his music, since it had been hammered out under
his feet for a month now. He was looking forward to
Eddie's plight and his hot meal.

He was going to be late for both occasions.

The men, the three of them he wanted to see, were
bunched together, coat collars up against the wind,
staring at the water. A string of half-loaded barges
lined the wharf-side. Convoy Wharf had survived the
war with no more than a few pockmarks where shrap-
nel from the AA guns had pitted it. It was a solid tes-
timony to the failure of the German blitz; ships had
continued to load and unload throughout the war.

Mainly now used for the unloading of paper, it occasionally saw the despatch of other cargoes.

The three men turned round as one when he walked up, staring at him with weatherbeaten, expressionless faces. Only the eyes gave an indication that they were observing him sharply, taking him all in.

No one would have guessed from their silent scrutiny that they had heard him coming, listened to his tread, and decided who he was and why he was there.

Only his name was lacking, and that they proposed to get out of him before giving him their own.

Coffin gave them no trouble here, he introduced himself at once.

'Thought we'd seen the last of you lot.' The speaker was a short, spare man with a forehead furrow set in a permanent frown.

'Had a couple of you round last week.' The second man was tall, thin and sad of face. His right hand was yellow with nicotine stains.

The third man was silent, but a faint, sceptical smile lifted his lips.

Coffin sighed, this was going to be slow. He got their names out of them. The first speaker was Jack Lash, the heavy smoker was Peter Peskett and the silent smiler was Paddy Flisker, and the smile was not a smile but a Celtic gesture of ambiguous intent.

What he wanted to get from them was a list of all the men who *might* have stolen the shoes, or possibly bought them from the original thief to hand on.

He had a list already, culled from the local police, but he wanted his own.

Even in his limited experience one name often led to another.

Between them, they produced a list of names in dribs and drabs. Quite soon he saw where it was heading.

Someone mentioned Alfred Arnold, who was a name on his list of suspects, someone else said casually he was married to an Italian girl called Leopardo.

Then someone else made a joke about Florrie the money-lender being a figure in their lives.

Leopardo—Padovani. There was the link.

They were all local men from Deptford and Rotherhithe, none from Greenwich, who might not realize the significance of what they were saying.

Or perhaps they did. There was a look about them, they were not innocent men, but tough and worldly in their own way.

John Coffin made careful notes, wrote down all the names and addresses, because he would have to make a report. But to him a clear signal had gone up.

He didn't know where it left him. How far could loyalty go?

Just because you had served with a chap, felt a liking for him and a lot of sympathy, should it influence you? Your judgement it could not touch, a thought welled up whether you desired it or not—but your behaviour?

The answer was no. But you could go slow. His present impulse was to go very slow indeed.

Then he heard the sound of pounding feet. Someone was running their way.

A man had come sprinting round the corner of Convoy Wharf, and he was shouting.

Coffin couldn't make out a word he was shouting, but understood all the same.

AS A VERY YOUNG ACTRESS Rachel Esthart had played in Sir James Barrie's one-act thriller, *Shall We Join the Ladies?*

The scene (there is but the one, and never a dénouement) is a dinner-party.

Whether by accident or design, Rachel had reproduced the atmosphere of that first act.

There they were, all the guests around the table, knowing that some doomful sentence was about to be pronounced upon them but not knowing yet what it was.

A strange company, they thought, as they looked around the table, but they had something in common: murder.

Inspectors Warwick and Banbury sat side by side. Chief Superintendent Dander was opposite. Wives had not been asked.

'A typical Rachel Esthart party,' Eddie Kelly had murmured. 'More men than women.'

He was across the table from Warwick and Banbury, and next to Chief Superintendent Dander.

Stella was there, and at the head of the table, Rachel herself.

On each side of her she had the two youngest men: Chris and Alex. Joan and Albie Delaney were at the foot of the table, side by side, seeking comfort from each other.

There was one empty chair: the one for John Coffin.

Florrie served the food, handing round the first course of ravioli, from the Padovani kitchen. Vic Padovani had brought it up himself and was in the kitchen finishing the rest of the meal; roast chicken with lemon sauce. His mood was not good. Every so often he surfaced to pour out the wine: Papa Padovani's best vintage.

At the head of the table Rachel appeared poised and calm. She was wearing a black and white silk print dress which Schiaparelli had made before the war.

Stella, studying her patron and hostess, was amazed at the skill with which Rachel was pushing back the past and entering the present. She could guess at the age of the dress from the quality of the silk (nothing of 'utility' about it) but Rachel had tightened the belt and lowered the neckline. Stella suspected a sharp study of the latest issue of *Vogue* in which the new Paris fashions were forecast. A new look was coming over clothes, you could sense it coming; Rachel had merely anticipated.

Suddenly, oddly, it was Rachel who was in tune with the times and Stella who felt out of touch.

After the ravioli, and while Vic was carving the chicken, Rachel started to talk:

'Dear friends.' She smiled, almost a threatening smile Stella felt. A waft of Ma Griffe floated from her, outdoing the smell of roast chicken and red wine.

No, not a threat in the smile, Stella decided, she's not got the feel of her audience yet and she's nervous.

Even as she watched she saw Rachel become confident, project herself.

'No,' she said. 'Not friends. You are not here as friends; you are here because I have a confession to make and you have come to hear it.'

Chief Superintendent Dander shifted on his chair.

Rachel took a swig of wine, smiled, a tentative, more normal smile now, and said: 'Well, to be honest, I thought I'd rather get it over in one throw. Tell you all at once.'

She rose, putting one hand on the table. 'The man who murdered the girl is no son of mine. I disown him. I will not have him. I won't let him contaminate the memory of the son I once had.'

'Sit down, ma'am,' said Dander kindly. 'You're overdoing yourself.'

He got up and held her chair.

Rachel hesitated for a moment, then sank down. Then she put out a hand, blindly seeking.

Dander took it. He looked embarrassed, but he did it.

Stella wanted to cheer. My God, she manages it still. What a performer. She's feeding them their parts.

'My child died years ago,' said Rachel. 'I know that now. I've known it for a long while in my heart, but I couldn't face it. Couldn't face the world. I hid in the nightmare I'd made.'

Dander relinquished her hand and went back to his seat. The look he exchanged with Warwick, alert, sharp, made Stella decide that he responded as a man but was on guard as a detective. He and Rachel were probably a match for one another.

Tom Banbury sat looking at Rachel without a word. She's learnt nothing and forgotten nothing, he thought, the silly cow. He was usually gentle in his thoughts but not now. His deeper mind was elsewhere. Tomorrow the trial of the murderer of Connie Shepherd would begin and end. The killer intended to plead guilty. Within the statutory time he would hang. Banbury could not get his mind out of the executioner's cell.

In a clear voice Rachel said: 'I was never lying, never acting a lie. I want you to believe that. When I first came back to Angel House I felt my child was still alive. It wasn't that I could not accept his death. To me it did not happen. He was still alive. I *knew* it.' She dropped her voice. 'Trauma, my psychiatrist called it. The result of shock.'

Joan Delaney put on her spectacles, thus transforming herself into a formidable lady. 'Now come on, Rachel. I know you, you've been coming round for some time now.'

'Yes. The war did that.' Rachel smiled wryly. 'Even hidden in Angel House I knew about the war. We had our bombs, too. As you so neatly put it, Joan, I was coming back. The *note*, the letter, threw me for a time. Just till the body. Not after that. I've seen my psychiatrist again, accepted treatment. I'll be ready to be out in the world again soon.'

There was silence.

'You understand what I'm doing? I'm apologizing and explaining. I have no son. He is dead. He died as a child. Years ago. I accept it.'

There was a noise outside and John Coffin came into the room.

He went straight to Dander and Warwick.

'Another body, sir. At Convoy Wharf. Found in the river. Stabbed like the last one. Only this time I knew her name: Shirley Cowley. But with the same message on her as before.'

He looked at Rachel. 'Sorry, Mrs Esthart.'

TEN

A SIGHT OF THE MURDERER'S HANDS

FOR ONE MOMENT John Coffin felt he held the ball in his hands, he was at the centre of the whole case. They were all listening to him; every word counted. Banbury, Warwick, even Chief Superintendent Dander. They were listening to *him*.

For a moment they were frozen into a position; the still life of a dramatic, devastating second.

Stella's face registered shock and surprise, but she retained enough presence of mind to go straight round to Rachel. They stood together in silence. Joan and Albie moved closer together with an instinctive timing. They didn't have to tell each other what their basic reaction was! Damn, this won't help the returns. Murder on the streets was a no-sale position.

Eddie Kelly and Chris Mackenzie froze into position as if this was a part of the play they had not rehearsed.

At this time he did not know Vic Padovani was present, because Vic was in the kitchen behind the door, listening, but he learnt later.

Then the scene broke into fragments, he caught snatches of conversation.

A phrase from the policemen, Warwick to Dander as they waited for the car:

'Mrs Esthart's scene; what did you make of that?'

'She was acting, of course.'

'Sure,' Warwick said. 'They all were.' He did not like actors.

'But she meant it for all that.'

'And she had something more to say. Not important, I doubt. But there was something else coming, I swear.' This was Dander again.

What had Rachel said? Coffin did not know yet. Something he had missed with his dinner.

The theatre group moved towards the door, as anxious now to leave, but for different reasons, as the three policemen.

Stella whispered in his ear. 'Come back as soon as you can. Here to Angel House. Rachel has something to say.'

To me! Coffin said to himself. Why to me?

He murmured something about being late.

'Never mind how late. It won't matter.'

Who was going to sleep tonight? Probably no policeman.

He didn't make a promise to Stella because he could not. Already he could see in Warwick's face that he was about to issue instructions to both Coffin and Alex Rowley.

When they came they amounted to no more than follow me and say nothing. He supposed he sounded like that to Eagle Scott, the laddie detective. There is a pecking order, boy, he decided, and you and I had better learn it. We are like utility furniture, you and I, we have our place, we are serviceable, but we are not greatly valued. You get us on a docket if you can show the need.

Feeling like a utility bed, he lumbered after his superiors.

Inspector Warwick had heard what Stella whispered, and before departing, said to John Coffin, 'So what's the old witch going to tell you? That she did the murder?'

'I don't think so, sir.'

'Know her well, do you?'

'Not really, sir.'

'And what about the girl?'

'A bit, sir.'

Warwick said, 'Well, let me know what she says.'

'Yes, sir.' If I can, sir. If I don't forget, sir.

Vic Padovani and Florrie were standing in the hall by the open front door. It was the first time Coffin realized Vic was present. Vic's face alarmed him.

He looked frightened. It was a look Coffin knew well; in their army days Vic had often been frightened. In battle, of course, but no more than most, only always when he had to say No. Vic hated saying No. He loved horses, dumb animals and kids.

'Vic?'

'What?'

'Oh well, nothing now. See you later, Vic.'

If you are a policeman on the outside, perhaps it is safer to stay that way and not try to get yourself and your friends inside anywhere.

'It's the same MO as before,' said Coffin to Alex on the way down. 'Same strangulation—manual, same stabbing and mutilation, and the card. Ditto, ditto. I saw, so I know. At the moment I know more than that lot.' He nodded towards the big police car, full of his superiors, rapidly disappearing down the hill. 'But that won't last.' It rankled.

His dark, black thought was prominent in his company as he walked down hill with Alex. No longer inchoate, it had taken on a shape, turning itself into a little animal or a bird which crouched upon his shoulders or sat upon his head. In either case it was unpleasant to look upon and better avoided. He remembered now that the migraines which had followed his war injury had sometimes, or so he felt, assumed an animal form; biting into his head with teeth. This feeling must be related, somehow.

A part of his recovery, but a nasty bit. But of course there was a reason for it, as there had been for the migraines. Something, not a bit of bone this time, but an awkward fact, was pressing on his mind. Alex saw this.

'It worries you?'

'I notice you are on the job this time and not sent off with Tom Banbury to check on infinitesimal bits of what might be the Shepherd child or her clothing.'

'That's because he hasn't got any. But as it happens, I'm not.' His tone was dry. 'I'm a kind of records clerk.'

The figure of the dead Shirley was going to absorb Coffin for a long time. Her hair, once so soft and curly, had fallen across her face in long strands. Her pretty dress was stained with blood and blotched with river muck. Her face was discoloured and swollen. As she had been dragged from the river he had made one quick examination to see the knife injuries to the genital area. For there the clothes had been removed. The stab wounds to the rest of the body were through the clothes.

He would not see her again. By now the body would be on its way to the mortuary in Greenwich, where the police surgeon would make his examination before handing over to a forensic team for further study.

But Coffin had seen enough.

Then he said what he had been wanting to say for some time. 'It was funny where the message card was attached this time.'

'Pinned to the brassiere?'

'That's it.'

'But it's understandable: no cardigan pocket. So it had to go somewhere that would protect it a bit.'

They carried on walking. At some point on that walk downhill to Greenwich the murderer was walking too, but it was too dark to see his face.

Two hours later a tired man climbed up the hill. He had spent the time on all the routine tasks of documentation and recording that fall to a junior detective.

He looked up at Angel House, praying that the lights would be out and he could walk on past. They were not, and he gave a small groan. All it needed now was for Eagle Scott to appear from the darkness.

In his exhaustion it suddenly seemed as if the whole evening had presented itself specially in drama form with carefully mounted scenes and he now had one more act to go, although afterwards he realized that this was not so and there was nothing unusual about it, just the mind doing its usual conjuring tricks of making order out of chaos, as if life was a story with a beginning and an end. Which it might not be.

Stella was waiting for him, on the lookout, and then Rachel.

They sat him in an armchair, then gave him whisky, which made him even sleepier than he was, thus turning Rachel's confession into something heard at a distance as through a tunnel, a small sound but very distinct. The verbal equivalent of a camera obscura.

In his state of semi-intoxicated, heightened awareness, she seemed a terrifying figure.

This figure was telling him that she had killed her own child. Let her son drown. This was what she had hidden from all these years, this the memory which for so long she had blacked out. This was the trauma of which her psychologist had so aptly spoken.

'You mustn't think I have known this all the time. In the beginning it was just as I told you. My son seemed still alive. But then, in bits, memories began to come back. Snatches. Little scenes, like the two of us having a picnic by a river, I was drinking wine. A lot, I suppose. Then a picture of him falling into the water. Someone was screaming. Me, it must have been. Just these bits, you see, that come back at intervals. I hated them. Didn't believe them.' She paused. 'Then one day, after one of the Blitzes, I saw the whole thing: myself on the river bank, the boy going in and never coming up. The current is very strong in that river at that place. It sucks you under. I saw myself leaving. I left the car, the picnic things. I took a train.' She was telling the tale in a monotone as if she had seen the whole thing like an old black and white film. 'I ran away and I have been running until now. Here I stop.'

Out of this tragedy, history had produced a murderer from Rachel Esthart, not from her womb but from her own psychosis.

Like Jack the Ripper he just arrived on the scene, nimble, quick and active for revenge.

In bed that night Coffin found a jingle running round his head.

> Jack be nimble, Jack be quick,
> When the rope swings, you will kick.
> Jack the tailor, soldier, sailor,
> Stranger, lodger, friend or neighbour,
> With every victim of your fun
> You show you are your mother's son.

ELEVEN

THE WAY THE MURDERER WALKED

THE MURDERER WAS OUT that night in the dark, not doing anything special, but retracing old footsteps, and thinking. Not worrying exactly; in this mood the murderer did not worry, or feel anxiety, only desire.

But he did not say to himself, What a good chap I am, how right in my doings, how satisfying in my skills. The mood of holy happiness that had sustained him during the murders was beginning to fray at the edges.

The murderer went down to the river. He liked water. It was cleansing, concealing, but also a means of transport. He was knowledgeable about the tides. There was no mystery about it: you could look them up. The passage of water up and down the Thames in response to the motions of the moon was regular and predictable. Every day had its twice high and low tides as measured from London Bridge. Seasonally, there are also exceptionally low tides called neap, and high known as spring.

On Thursday, May 3, the high tide had been 2.54 a.m., and 3.17 p.m., as measured at London Bridge, some fifteen minutes later at Greenwich. On May 11, the tide was running some three hours earlier.

He had absorbed this knowledge before he knew what use he would make of it. Indeed, it was because he knew, the use ensued. It came to his hand, as it were.

It would not be true to say that anything might be grist to his mill, but he was, so to speak, a creative murderer. In which he would surprise the detectives chiefly concerned, Inspector Warwick and Chief Superintendent Dander, who believed that killers like this did not alter their modus operandi.

In one crucial respect his presentation of the murders changed: he added an extra detail, but they do not know that yet. He himself is not aware how illuminating this difference will be to one mind closely attuned to his own. This is because the murderer is sensitive to himself but not to other people, whom he consistently underrates. Not so that they notice, he is quite bright, but underneath he does not think that most people he meets and works with are as clever as he is himself.

Deep inside himself, he realized that the matter of the black-market shoes worn by Shirley and Eileen and Lorna pointed towards him. He did not mind this pointer. In his arrogance he wanted, in a way, to be known.

To be known and yet not to be known: that was his game. He wanted to parade himself, give the pursuers a pointer, yet to dance ahead, forever elusive. He thought he hid himself rather well.

If he did not elude the chase then he knew what lay ahead: death by hanging.

TOM BANBURY was still thinking again about the execution room and the condemned cell; he wished he could shed the thought. The only comfort he had was that people could not see inside his face so they did not know what he was thinking.

He was a working policeman and as such was well aware that there was something selective about his present position. His workload was surprisingly light. He was being sheltered. Or pushed aside. He reached out his hand for the whisky bottle.

It was a pity Dander knew about the whisky.

He took up a file of papers connected with other tasks such as the security of the royal family while in Greenwich, Greenwich Hythe and Greenwich Wick. Plenty of crooks, few traitors, was how he expressed it. The King and Queen were more in danger of having their pockets picked than being shot at.

Finishing his drink, he went to bed, a business easily accomplished by him these days as he simply took off some clothes and crawled under the sheets. His stepmother, whom he disliked, came in once a week to clean. She called it her service to God. Banbury sometimes got the impression she disliked God as much as she disliked him and he disliked her.

Tonight he didn't sleep. He kept company with all his dead.

ALL THE PADOVANI FAMILY slept like the dead, Vic among them. But he, poor lad, had one idiosyncrasy, he shouted in his sleep. His mates in the army, Coffin among them, could bear witness to this.

On the night of Rachel's party, when so many others were restless, he was asleep but bellowing.

His father came and shook his head, which was the family's technique for arousing him.

'You're at it again. That's too much of it lately.'

'I thought I was walking,' said the wretched Vic. 'Up and down, up and down, by the river with weights on my feet.' He didn't say he had the double murders on his mind, but he had.

'Stay awake, then, and give us some peace.'

Papa Padovani departed: he had his own worries, such as black-market shoes and the tenor of the Food Inspector's report on the nature of his wine. Mama Padovani stayed awake; she was worried that she might know the identity of the murderer.

IN ANGEL HOUSE, Rachel Esthart, purged of her guilt at last, slept like the angel on the roof. She was worn out, exhausted, temporarily dead to the world.

But inside vitality was bubbling. She had plans. These plans no longer included Stella.

EDDIE KELLY was among those others not sleeping well.

He had a smart flat within easy driving distance of the Theatre Royal, Nelson Street, where he now sat in a striped dressing-gown, smoking an Abdullah. 'Doing his Noel Coward act,' was how he expressed it.

He had the sense that one period of his life was drawing to an end and another about to begin.

The time at the Theatre Royal had been formative, shaping. His life after would never be the same; but it was time to move on.

He would miss Stella Pinero. He had loved her more than he would ever admit, but she was not his future. He hoped she would not mind. Probably not. A tough young lady.

As for Rachel Esthart, she had laid hands upon his life and marked it. He'd be glad to leave her behind. If he could do. If. He had an idea Rachel was stronger than he guessed.

He lit another cigarette. It was time for relationships to end, time to go.

OTHER CHARACTERS from the Theatre Royal were having a restless night. Chris was trying to compose music in his mind. Silent music. Beethoven could do it, why not Chris? But Chris couldn't. Too many emotions were wavering inside.

Love. Hate. Despair.

Bloody, bloody women, he thought, and wanted to kick the wall. But that would waken Mrs Lorimer who slept next door.

He got up and started to carve a bird, a seagull.

JOAN AND ALBIE SHARED a double bed as they had done all their married life. Perhaps each had had adventures outside the marriage-bed but they had been passing: their relationship with each other and the theatre was what counted.

Joan whispered, 'We're nearly done, aren't we? Funny, isn't it? Six months ago we had a profit and today we're in the red. That's theatre for you. Why do we bother? Why *do* we bother?' She shook her sleepy husband. 'Albie—I can think of how we could raise money. And it might be a whizz. A risk, though.' Albie did not answer, and Joan lay on her back, thinking. I think the Queen would like it, she decided. A compliment, really. If I worked it right.

IN MRS LORIMER'S Coffin eventually slept lightly and uncomfortably. He had the feeling too much life was stirring in the house below, who was still up and around?

He too feared that he knew the identity of the murderer. In the water the third yet first body drifted free, and floated upwards. An early worker, a stevedore, saw her there as the summer dawn made the water rosy. He looked in horror at the face rising to the top of the water. It was a face, recognizably a woman's face.

The third, last, yet first body had arrived. The tiny woman who had crouched in the recess in the stone river wall of the Isle of Dogs had finally come floating free. The belt of her dress which had caught her there on a piece of projecting metal had rotted apart. She was loose. Eileen Gaze was floating at last.

The stevedore telephoned the police and then the local newspaper. This man had an instinctive grasp of the needs of the situation. The newspaper office was closed at that hour, but he knew the home number of the girl reporter. 'Here, Julia, I've got this for you.'

The girl listened with interest, making notes. 'Yes, I've got that. I know the place. I'll be down there. Have the police got there yet? No? Good. I'll bring a photographer. If I can.' She kept her fingers crossed.

She went on keeping her fingers crossed. There was so much going on: a royal visit with the King and Queen and the two princesses. Someone had said Queen Mary was coming also. A masque to be performed by the local rep. And incidentally a strong rumour that the Delaneys were going bust and would be replaced by Michael Redgrave. The reporter, Julia Fawcett, who hoped to write plays, took a keen interest in this.

Also the hunt for the Shepherd daughter. Her mother's murderer was a local man, and Julia was preparing a piece, an obituary if you like, to be published when he was hanged.

There was almost too much happening. 'Thanks, dad,' she said affectionately. 'First with the news, eh?'

Jack the Ripper is not a gothic figure, he does not walk the castle of the mind. He is industrial man, an urban murderer. He needs the streets, the tenements.

In particular he needs the newspapers, the radio, because he wants to be heard.

TWELVE

THE FACE OF THE MURDERER

BREAKFAST at Mrs Lorimer's was tea and burnt toast with Mrs Lorimer crying quietly into her teacup. All over Greenwich women were about to ask themselves if their husband, brother, lover or parent was this terrible murderer of women. Each of them chose the man they loved and feared most. Mrs Lorimer thought she *knew*.

The news spread very quickly from mouth to mouth, growing all the time. Soon there were four murderers, five, six.

Breakfast at Angel House was coffee and crisp, fresh toast. Stella made it and brought it on a tray to where Rachel sat enthroned in bed. When the telephone rang, Stella went into the hall to answer it.

'Stella? I'm glad I've got you. There's been another body in the river.'

'Another. *Yet* another?'

'A third. You'd better tell Rachel.'

'Is it the same sort of killing? Are you sure? Where are you speaking from?' She could hear noises which did not sound like a police station but did sound like Lady Olivia.

'Lorimer's. And I am sure.' He looked down to see Eagle Scott give a toothy grin. 'I've been told I have it from a totally reliable source.'

He started to put the receiver down. A kind of keening noise was coming from upstairs. Unmistakable in origin.

'For God's sake quieten that woman,' he said to his landlady.

Mrs Lorimer took up a tray of tea and sacrificial toast. 'Lady Olivia, dear,' he heard, before the door closed.

Stella said, 'John—this means something terrible, doesn't it? I can tell by your voice.'

'Then you can tell more than I can.' But he had had a bad feeling for a long time, and now it was back sitting like a big black bird on his shoulder. Like Mama Padovani, like Mrs Lorimer, he thought he knew the murderer. 'Where will you be all today?'

'Need you ask? The theatre. Rehearsing, fitting dresses for the Masque.'

At these words a faint pleasure stirred in Coffin's mind. 'Is it true that Eddie Kelly fell in the water last time you rehearsed?'

'True and somewhat; he fell in twice.' Like the loyal little trouper she was, she did not reveal that Eddie's toupé fell off in the water and had to be retrieved like a wet rat. Eddie had looked like murder and it certainly took your mind off sex.

Eagle Scott looked at him eagerly. 'It's interesting, isn't it? Will you see the body?'

'Yes.' He would if he could, but would he be pushed to the perimeter again? There was a glass wall all around him, like one of those bells inside which the Victorians placed flower arrangements.

He had a sudden picture of himself sitting, a little mannikin, on a satin cushion. He was not alone inside the glass bell; he had a companion in there with him, as had become increasingly obvious. The murderer was in there with him.

IT WAS A HOT DAY. Flags were already going up on houses in Greenwich. Pictures of the King and Queen, he in uniform, she in pale blue and pale fur, appearing in all windows. Every so often there was a picture of Winston Churchill, cigar and V sign complete. There were no pictures of Clement Attlee even where the householder had voted Labour. In Greenwich Hythe there was a solitary picture of Stalin. The elderly, almost blind widow who lived there believed it to be a portrait of General Montgomery. No one liked to tell her otherwise.

Every available policeman, both plain-clothes and uniformed branch was working. All leave was cancelled, and as Sergeant Tew said bitterly (it was his wedding anniversary and a treat for him and his wife had been planned), you had to be mortally ill even to get a dinner break.

There was no fresh evidence about the missing Sybil Shepherd. The murderer of her mother continued to affirm he knew nothing. Tom Banbury was beginning to believe him. He put the case aside temporarily, thus leaving his energies free for other activities.

He made the self-comment that he seemed to be considered a safe man in dealing with the royal family. He gave himself a wry good mark. In the course of these duties he flushed out several old friends. He was almost glad to see them: con men and pickpockets were not killers. Violence was anathema to them, all they wanted was a little quiet money.

A dull anger sat inside his stomach, causing him pain which he communicated to those he worked with. Alex Rowley felt it most, but Coffin came in for his share. Chief Superintendent Dander recognized the mood, he had met the pale shadow of it in his wife. His own mood became harder.

He went into yet another conference with Warwick from which both emerged silent and grim.

Details about the new victim were coming in quickly. She was a married woman, mother of one child, whose husband had been in Germany in the army of occupation, and she was believed to have left home for a lover. She had been identified by her sister and sister-in-law, who had come to the police station in Greenwich together. The husband was there now being questioned. He was obviously a prime suspect.

Except for certain matters that Warwick and Dander were, as yet, keeping to themselves.

It was midday, on Monday, after the discovery of the third body. Dander was thirsty. Also angry with himself.

'A drink? At the Ragman's, across the road?'

The Ragman was the local name for the Duke of York pub. The origin of the name was wrapped in mystery.

'If you like.' Warwick wasn't keen. 'I suppose they've got some beer?'

'They've usually got it when no one else has.'

Even beer was in short supply. But policemen could usually find some. Publicans knew whom to look after.

'Is it time to talk to Banbury? Have a word?'

'No.'

'I think it is.'

'No, I know Tom Banbury and you don't. We'd do no good. And might do harm. Besides...'

'What?'

'Don't you think he *knows* what's up?'

Warwick sipped his beer. 'Yes,' he said slowly. 'Yes. For sure he does.' Be a fool if he didn't, a professional policeman as he was. 'You're right. We've kept him out. On the edge, but he knows what's going on.' He shrugged. 'We've got a suspect.'

Both men had separately and together interviewed the husband of Eileen Gaze and the parents of Shirley Cowley.

The point in common that all the women had was The Padovani, and the Theatre Royal, Nelson Street.

AT THE THEATRE ROYAL, Nelson Street, Joan Delaney was discovering with relief that returns were not down, the inhabitants of Greenwich were not giving up the theatre on account of the murder (perhaps they felt safer there), and that the rest of London was apparently anxious to take seats. The telephone never stopped ringing.

She decided to postpone the production of *Twelfth Night* and put in *Night Must Fall*.

If horror was what the fans wanted, they could have it.

Meanwhile, the Masque was coming on well. Eddie had learnt to manage his boots and his hair, there was no danger he would fall into the river again, while Stella was enchanting.

She herself was to play the Queen, a much more taxing part, and a treat she deserved after all her self-denial that season in bringing in outside stands for London and letting Stella and Bluebell show off. The audiences loved them, but she knew they were showing-off.

They might go bankrupt, but, by God, they would die in style.

Besides, on that issue, she had plans.

Joan forgot the murders. She had no worries about Albie who had worked by her side every day, almost never out of her sight, and slept at night in their old double bed as he always had.

About Eddie Kelly and Chris Mackenzie, whom she had some reason to think had almost certainly been otherwise disposed, except as touched her theatre, she did not care at all.

Two DAYS into the investigation of the new deaths, plus Lorna Beezley, now centred on a suite of special

offices in the Greenwich police station with a newly
installed Nissen hut (ex RAF stores) in what had been
the school playground. The main school building was
undergoing major rebuilding and there was brickdust
everywhere. There were similar sub-offices on suit-
able spots in Greenwich Hythe and Greenwich Strand.
It was a circus, with an air of slight madness about it,
but an organized one.

Chief Superintendent Dander and Inspector Warwick presided over a meeting in which all the information coming in was pooled and discussed with the
investigating policemen, now a large team.

Attention was focused most sharply on the two new
victims Shirley Cowley and Eileen Gaze, a married
woman of twenty-five, and the only one of the three
to have borne a child.

Smoking was allowed.

The air was heavy with Player's and Gold Flake
within the first ten minutes. Dander was reputed to
smoke Balkan Sobranies but never did so in public.
Instead he chewed on a dead pipe which he used like a
musical instrument.

The tune he was playing was one they all knew, a
complicated little melody in a low key.

How were the victims killed? How had their iden-
tities been established?

The points came quick and fast; each girl had been
strangled, then attacked with a knife. Repeatedly
stabbed, mutilated. In each case the instrument had
been a pointed blade, sharpened on both sides. In each
case the manner of attack had great similarities.

Eileen Gaze had been dead for some two weeks before the other girls. She had died almost as soon as she had disappeared from her home.

Coffin heard a voice, his own, say, 'Is it correct, sir, that *no* card was found on the body of Mrs Gaze.'

Warwick was succinct. 'No, no card was found. There may have been one that was washed away, but the forensics have no evidence—pin holes and such—to suggest there was.'

Eileen Gaze had died well before the others, but held no card addressed to Rachel Esthart. This was the great difference.

The thought that came was interesting, but terrible. The black creature, bird or beast, on his shoulder stirred.

Warwick's brisk catalogue continued: what contacts could be established for the dead woman in the big wide world of London, such as what boyfriends, employers, enemies and neighbours? It was for them to find out. Even the man she sat next to on the No. 10 bus if they could trace him.

Did they know each other? And if so, where and how and at one point did their paths come close and cross?

There was a map of Greenwich, Greenwich Hythe and Greenwich Wick. Marked on it were points where the girls had been known: different colours for each girl.

Yellow for Lorna Beezley.

Red for Shirley Cowley.

Blue for Eileen Gaze.

The yellow and red dots were concentrated more or less in one area, with more perhaps in the Hythe for Shirley who had lived there, but the blue points were all over the place.

Eileen had got about a bit.

Which was what her sister-in-law had complained, and the police could now confirm.

From his seat tucked away at the back of the room from where he could see the board and the back of Alex Rowley's neck, Coffin thought: pattern of their lives, that's what I'm looking at. Jazzy little affairs, too. Shirley's looked like a comet with a couple of tails, Eileen's more like an octopus.

Dance halls, cinemas, shops and hairdresser, these were places they had frequented.

Did their paths cross anywhere? Warwick had asked the question and now answered himself.

'Yes. They crossed at several points.' Coffin saw the back of Alex's neck go red.

'There were at least three places where all three women went.' Banbury pointed to the map. 'The Padovani Restaurant in Church Row, the Theatre Royal, Nelson Street, in Lower Greenwich Street, and the Rose-dream Dance Hall in the Woolwich Road. They may have met, they may not. As yet we don't know.'

Shirley and Eileen had danced at the Rose-dream, where Lorna Beezley had sometimes played in the band. She too loved to go dancing. Shirley had served food at The Padovani where Eileen and Lorna had eaten and drunk. All of them had sat in the audience to watch the company perform at the theatre, and

Shirley and Lorna had gone back-stage. Possibly Eileen had as well.

Coffin focused again on what Warwick was saying:

'The killer, the multiple killer of all these women—because we are, at this moment, assuming one killer to be responsible—is someone with pronounced characteristics. He will be weak, but might think himself strong, and will probably have inherited a difficult relationship with both his parents.

'I say we must go looking for someone who has been damaged by life. Someone angry, hurt, feeling inferior, but inside him conscious of being superior. That is the man we are looking for.'

Warwick had delivered himself of the most profound intellectual statement of his life, and he was as red in the face as Alex's neck: a striking match.

Warwick was answering a question: 'Yes, we have some suspects, but no positive names.'

Lying bugger, thought Coffin. You have a name. Must have. I have myself. But he did not blame his senior officer for not naming names.

The meeting broke up without him having contributed to it, but he had not been meant to, and had not been trying.

He stood at the door looking at Alex Rowley. Tom Banbury brushed past them.

'Cut off to work, you two,' he said brusquely.

'He's angry,' said Alex.

'Upset more.' Coffin had long since decided Tom Banbury was a more emotional man than he'd realized at first, always a lot more going on underneath than you thought. 'The Shepherd case dug into him.'

'Think so?'

'Yes. I could see it. Didn't see it at first, but I do now. Me as well. And you, too.'

Alex did not answer.

No reply given and none expected.

He was in a wicked mood himself, thought Coffin.

Leaving Alex to his own plans, he slipped out the back way through what had once been the caretaker's flat, in the days when the place had been a school. An iron gate led straight into a side street.

As he got there a police car drew up, Vic Padovani got out with two plain-clothes detectives from Inspector Banbury's elite.

John Coffin drew back behind the gate. He didn't want Vic to see him. Nor did he wish to meet Vic's eyes.

Damn, he thought, did it have to be Vic?

HE NEEDED TO TALK things over with someone. Not Stella, not Alex, not yet.

He loved Stella, but he could not involve her in this, his own private investigation.

If it came to Dander's or Warwick's notice that he was running a little private operation of his own he would probably be drummed out. No, that was an archaic army expression, not to be used.

But you had a responsibility to a pal.

All right, you suspected a chap you'd served with of murder, a series of nasty murders; but you also had a duty to see if you could clear him. It was better, in the peculiar circumstances, to be unobtrusive, and to any former dweller in Hookey Street melting away into the background was easy.

He had come to Greenwich in a hopeful mood, looking forward to finding a brother or a sister; intending to set up a good relationship with the boss, Tom Banbury, and make good pals like Alex Rowley. Finding Vic Padovani there had looked like a bonus. Falling in love with Stella had been unexpected, a joy, whatever came of it.

But now it was all going sour. Murder was not just the affair of the murderer and the victim; no, it infected all it touched. He felt as sick himself as anyone.

Going about his business, he found himself later that day looking in men's outfitters, Purdey and Son, Happy Rise, Blackheath, established in 1880.

My grandpa would have been alive then, he thought, wonder if he ever shopped here? Dimly he recalled a spry, lame old fellow wearing a smart bowler. The rest of his clothes might not have been elegant but, as he put it himself, he liked a smart titfer.

Anthony Edens were more the thing now; Coffin contemplated their suave sleek lines wistfully before he decided they would not go with his ears. As well to be honest about your faults.

'Mr Coffin, sir!'

It was Eagle Scott. Yes, clearly Eagle Scott today and not Paul Shanks.

'Good name for a detective, sir.' He was in a cheeky mood.

'It's Cornish,' said Coffin briefly. He disliked jokes on his name.

'You Cornish, sir?'

'No. Don't you ever go to school?'

'Dinner-time, sir. Just on my way back.'

Glib little beast. Probably playing hookey. He wasn't the person to confide in, too young by a quarter of a century, but he was a lad with a golden touch for murder. Some future there.

When you'd met him things happened. So it was now. Nothing planned, not a purpose, the boy just had a natural gift for moving things on.

Perhaps it was telepathy or telekinesis or one of those strange things they investigated at Duke University in 1946.

Or even something to do with time. Coffin had read Dunne's Theory of Time, and been to see *Time and the Conways* at the Theatre Royal, Nelson Street. He hadn't understood it but he'd enjoyed it.

'Just been down to the *Kentish Mercury* to get a job as a junior reporter.' Eagle Scott, *né* Paul Shanks, had abandoned any pretence of going back to school.

'Did they give you one?' Boy detective, junior reporter. Quite a career structure, this lad was building.

'No. Got a Saturday job, though, sorting back issues.' He danced a sort of jig.

'Suppose you're still on the detection game as well?'

'Oh yes. Rather. Looking up the back files on Mrs Esthart, too.'

Later, Coffin was to wonder if Eagle Scott was really a sort of phantom who appeared only to transmit information, then disappeared again. Someone with supernatural powers it would be as well to keep an eye on.

'Thanks, Eagle. You've been a help.' He passed a coin across. 'Keep in touch, Eagle.'

You bring me ideas. In fact, two.

'Where are you going, boss?'

That boy went to too many American gangster films. He looked at his watch, nearly midday. He bade a mental goodbye to the check he was doing on the cheap lodging-houses of the area and decided to pursue his own inquiry.

A BUS RIDE to the *Kentish Mercury* offices near Deptford Broadway and a lot of thinking to do.

No one on the crowded bus was talking about the murders, but much conversation was about the shortage of potatoes, the nastiness of the bread and the wet summer.

As he entered the quiet, dark, front office of the *Kentish Mercury*, he felt a sense of relief. He was doing the right thing.

He introduced himself and produced his credentials. He wasn't hiding who he was, and explained his purpose.

'Oh yes,' the pretty, dark girl behind the counter was anxious to help. Curious too, but asking no questions. The war was still close enough for the instructions, Careless Talk Costs Lives, still to mean something. 'You can see what you want. Recent editions will it be? Just say.'

'No. Not recent.' He liked the face, she wasn't as pretty as Stella but her face had a solid sweetness to it. 'No, not recent at all. Fourteen years back.'

Her eyes opened wide as she listened to what he wanted.

'Oh yes. I can find them. But you'll have to wait. And they'll be dirty. We had a rocket across the way and we got all the dust.'

'I'll wait.'

He lit a cigarette, drew up a chair, ready to take what came.

After a quick look at him, the girl produced a cup of coffee. 'Here. No sugar, we're short, but the coffee is good. I make it myself.'

He sipped it while he waited. The sun had come out to warm his back.

Eventually the girl appeared to lead him to an inner room where a stack of dusty, yellowing papers were laid out on a table. 'You can work here. I'll bring you some more coffee. You'll need it.'

It was quite a pile, the *Mercury* was a weekly, but paper had not been rationed then, in those pre-war days. He tried a joke:

'I should have brought something to read.'

He drew up a chair to the table and started work.

As he had expected, the *Mercury* had covered the tragedy of Rachel Esthart and her son thoroughly over the weeks.

The case had fallen into three parts. The first when Rachel Esthart and her son had been missed from their home. No direct comments in this part about why she had disappeared, but strong hints of a quarrel with her husband. The headlines in this early chapter were such as ACTRESS DISAPPEARS, or THEATRE STAR MISSING FROM HOME.

The pictures of Rachel looked more dated than he would have expected. It really was a far away scene, that pre-war world. Seemed more antique and dead than Queen Anne.

The second stage could be briefly headed: Where is the child? Rachel had been found, wandering, apparently amnesiac and shocked. But she was alone. This stage ended with the discovery of the drowned boy.

The third stage began with the inquest on the boy. Subsequently came the series of events which might be called the Trial by Ordeal of Rachel Esthart. Did she drown her son? No, the verdict was accidental drowning, apparently supported by the medical evidence. Well, then, everyone was asking what had Rachel been about when her son was drowned.

John Coffin now knew the answer. Or the answer according to Rachel. She had let him drown. But he thought behind this terrible confession must be some other trauma of which even Rachel herself might not be aware. But he would not play psychologist, that was not his purpose.

THE REPORTS WERE FULL and detailed, containing many pictures, some photographs, some line drawings.

There was an interview with the policeman who had handled the investigation in Oxfordshire of the missing boy. Rachel had turned up in Burford. The boy's body had been found in the Thames near Lechlade. Inspector Malcom had handled the case, but the first policeman to view the dead boy had been Police Constable Charles King. From his description you could tell the body was in a bad state, so that if Rachel refused to admit it was her son there was a reason. PC King, a family man himself, as he said, had sounded upset.

The London end of the investigation had been in the hands of Inspector Billy House, whose name was still treasured among South London policemen as that of a grand eccentric. Sergeant Black and a young detective called Banbury had their names mentioned.

There was a picture of Rachel, of her husband, very handsome, in a matinée-idol style. Also one of Eddie Kelly, looking very young and boyish. Very handsome, too.

John Coffin replaced the papers and said goodbye to the pretty girl.

It might seem crazy, but he thought he had found what he was looking for. He needed a bit more research. Just for his own sake there were some questions to ask.

And there was a marvellous bonus. In the post-August Bank Holiday, 1937, edition of the newspaper he had found a picture of William Alfred Clarke, Butcher, photographed outside his home with his prize greyhound, Wellington. His address was given: 23 Abbey Gardens, Charlton.

CLUTCHING HIS NOTES, John Coffin emerged into the sunlight. A memory of a man called Will Summers, talking to him stirred. He had spoken to Will Summers (who had seen the first body in the water) and got the impression that Will was telling him something.

He had forgotten all about it, but now seemed the time to find out. It was always tricky finding a lighterman on the river, they came and went with the tide, but luck was with him. He located Will in a pub called the Trafalgar Tavern. He was sitting alone, drinking from a pewter pot.

Will looked up, showed no signs of recognizing John Coffin (although Coffin felt reasonably sure that he had), and returned to his beer.

John took his own pewter pot over and put it on the table. 'Hello.'

'Oh, it's you.'

'That's right.' He sat down. 'Something to ask.'

Will remained silent, so John went on. He sipped his beer and quietly went over the conversation he had had on that first day with the man; where necessary, he consulted his notes. Will remained expressionless. 'And so,' concluded John, 'I somehow got the impression you were telling me something.' Will did not dispute it. But he did not add to it, either. 'So what was it? Come on, now, I mean to know.'

Reluctantly Will said, 'Saw one of you lot around the place earlier on, week before, didn't I? More than once. Struck me as odd. A look at the river—anyone might—not too often, though.'

'One of *us*? A policeman, then? So who was it?'

'Can't tell you his name,' said Will with a blank face. But there was a look in his eyes that spoke for him.

Coffin stood up. 'Thanks. You already have.'

THE PADOVANI was closed when Coffin walked past on his way to Angel House. A notice on the door said simply:

'Closed owing to absence of the proprietor.'

So it looked as though Papa Padovani had been taken in as well.

The Padovani might be closed, but Angel House was opening up. Curtains were drawn back, and the rooms inside were undergoing a spring-cleaning.

He did not have to ask for Rachel Esthart because she opened the door to him. 'Poor old Padovanis,' she said. 'Your lot seemed to have collared them all.'

'Ma as well?'

'No, she's in bed with a migraine. Florrie is ministering.' She was wearing a dark blue dress with penny-sized white dots, achieving, without effort, an up-to-date elegance.

'Where's the dog?' The old Rachel always carried her pet.

'In the garden.'

'Things are changing round here.' A coldish wind was blowing through all the open windows. At least the old Angel House had been cosy. This new one felt as though it might be going to be brisk and nipping.

'Just an airing. Not before time. This is work, I suppose, not social?' Coffin nodded. 'Well, I'm telling you: Vic Padovani is not a murderer.'

'We don't know.' And it was true, he did not know what evidence Vic was busily hanging around Vic's neck. The black-market shoes, the beetroot wine stain on the cards. He'd known the girls, or two of them. There might be more circumstantial evidence he was not aware of.

But only circumstantial, murders like these had no witnesses, no alibis, and circumstantial evidence could be wrong.

'Could we have a talk?' Rachel made an inarticulate noise. It occurred to Coffin, she wasn't good at writing her own dialogue. Or her own parts. It sounded like, No, I don't see why, but he ignored it. 'Going right back. Some questions to ask.' Then he thought again. 'No, no questions.' He took her by the hand and led her into the next room and sat her down on a chair. This is a great and gracious lady, he told himself, treat her like one. 'Just talk, ma'am, if you will. Tell me what it was like?' She looked at him, huge, pale eyes. 'Tell me what it was like, as you remember, when the boy was found. It's the killing ground, ma'am, that's what we call it in the army. From what you tell me of that time, we may help Vic and find the killer.' Then he added honestly. 'I'm just guessing.'

He hesitated, then said: 'To begin with, tell why you think it happened to you? What started it off?'

She was silent.

'I know they say you quarrelled with your husband. That there was violence between you. That you were drinking. Drugs, too, perhaps? But that's not all. It's connected with Edward Kelly, isn't it?'

He knew he'd struck home. 'He was your lover?'

Slowly Rachel said: 'He was not my lover: he was my husband's. Eddie was seduced by my husband. I don't blame Eddie. Or not much.'

The cork was out of the bottle.

Where she had once forgotten, now she remembered all. Out of the deep-frozen memory, it all came pouring, newly minted, fresh. Every detail.

A vivid description of the dead boy whom she could not recognize, even his clothes were stained and dirtied beyond knowing. Yes, she recalled the policeman in Oxfordshire. Not the older man so clearly, but the younger one. He'd been sympathetic, he had a son himself. The wife was a termagant though, a natural bully. 'How did I come to see the wife, I wonder? She must have given me a cup of tea or something. I think people tried to be kind. Yes, I remember so well. Now.'

Coffin prompted her. 'And in London?'

'Oh yes, and poor Tom Banbury. So young and so taut. He was miserable, you know. Brought up unhappily. I don't think he has ever forgiven me. Hates me.'

'No, oh no. Not that,' said Coffin.

'It's all my fault.'

There it was again, that self-obsessed side. She needed to be slapped out of it.

'No. You won't like this, Rachel Esthart, but it is not your fault. I'd call you crucial but not essential to the murders. The murderer knew you and your troubles years ago. He never forgot you. I'd say you fascinated him. But you did not cause the murders. Nor did your son, God rest his soul. You are only the icing on the cake that was baked in another oven.'

You are part of the furniture of the murderer's mind, Rachel Esthart; in the end, it was nothing to do with you.

'What about the cards, then?'

'I'm not sure. A bit of fun, I think. The murderer's little giggle.'

Slowly Rachel said, 'The cards were so like my own. Do you think they *were* my cards? I could have missed some.'

'No,' he said thoughtfully. 'Not yours, but chosen perhaps because he could have known you had such cards. They're common enough but I just have this feeling.' The feeling that nothing this murderer did was by chance. He wanted to involve Rachel Esthart, to degrade her any way he could, a slow, spiritual murder. He's inventive, this murderer.

'But that means—' She stopped.

'Yes, he is someone who knows you. Sees you.' Then he added gently, 'But that always seemed likely, didn't it?'

There had been no stain on Rachel's supply of cards. But he knew how the murderer's cards could have found a stain.

'What about the seagull?'

'I'm not sure about the seagull.'

For a moment disquiet stirred within him as he remembered the seagull. That suggested more than spiritual murder.

THE TWO CHIEF POLICEMEN concerned with the investigation, Dander and Warwick, were talking over a glass of beer in Dander's local.

Stripped of the persona which their young policeman Coffin had deposited all over them like paint, the qualities which he thought he saw, they were two tired, troubled, middle-aged men. They had been considering the forensic report delivered that day which dealt with the deposit scattered on all the victims.

Brickdust, cement, and a powdering of plaster and rust.

On each victim similar deposits had been found. Identical fragments had been found on the clothing quietly abstracted from the locker of a prime suspect.

It was true that many Londoners might have a similar deposit on their clothing just now, because of all the rebuilding. But deposits are as individual as fingerprints to the trained eye. The murderer was thus marked; he had left his spoor behind.

'So what do we do? Go in and get him? All the evidence is circumstantial.'

'Personal observation.' Watch him, he meant.

'Yes.' Dander drank some more. 'We're in a privileged position.'

'Sorry.' He sounded sincere.

'Oh, don't think I mind.' And yet he did. Professional pride came into it. Loyalty, too. What kind of a policeman enjoys the destruction of another? 'Poor old Tom Banbury.'

Warwick was silent, he was not so personally involved. All he wanted was a case that would go to the Director of Public Prosecutions and stand up. Of course, it had its unpleasant side. He thought Dander was overdoing the charity bit.

They sat in silence. Dander said at last, 'It's hard on the young ones.' He was thinking of the war, of dangers faced, death survived. The person who went into battle wasn't the same one who came out. You just couldn't tell what violence given and endured could do to a man. He'd look out for the young ones. It was really part of his job, and he ought to take it more seriously. He liked that cocky young one with the unlikely name. 'Better get home,' he said without enthusiasm. He had nothing much to get home to.

STELLA EMERGED from the little hut set aside as a dressing-room in the grounds of the Naval College. It had been a disastrous rehearsal down on the barge. Chris's music, played on a flute and recorder, had sounded weak, Eddie had quarrelled with Chris, Chris had quarrelled with Albie, Stella had quarrelled with the wardrobe-room girl, and on the theory of it never rains but it pours, Albie had been bloody to all of them. Everyone had stalked off in a temper.

It had been a tense, restless day with people crowding her all the time. The police had been around the theatre asking questions about the black-market shoes which they had all been buying from Vic Padovani. She had seen Alex talking to Bluebell, who was in tears. Stella herself had escaped to her dressing-room.

This brought her to a faint worry: the letter she had written to her best friend had gone from her make-up box. Silly of her to keep it there.

In this letter she had named a man she feared. But he couldn't be the killer.

She was on her own. Outside the gates of the old palace she saw a small boy with a box Brownie trying to photograph her. She gave him a radiant smile and a piece of her chocolate ration. It was all a game; she knew there was no photograph because you couldn't get film. The RAF had it all. But it was practice for when she had fans.

Then she walked straight into the arms of a man.

'Whoa, Stella,' he said. 'Watch where you're going.'

'Just walking home.' She was half glad to see him, for she did not like the dark, and half not, for she was not seeking his company.

'I'll come with you. You're all jittery.' He took her by the arm.

'I've been quarrelling; it always upsets me. I need calming down.'

But not permanently, not for ever.

AFTER HIS TALK with Rachel Esthart, John Coffin looked for Alex, who he could not find, so he left a couple of notes. He tried to talk to Stella at the theatre, but Bluebell came to the phone instead to say breathlessly that she could not find Stella. 'She'll be back soon,' went on Bluebell happily. 'I'll tell her you want her. *Everyone's* after her today.' Bluebell had already answered one query. 'But I know where she is: rehearsing a scene for the Masque on the barge with Eddie Kelly.' She giggled. 'Rehearsing to Chris's music. He's down there too. And won't the fur fly.'

'Stella fond of Eddie, isn't she?' asked Coffin with sudden intuition.

'Was, dear, was. You are out of date. It's been Chris for some time now.'

And where does that leave me? Coffin asked himself with a desolate feeling. Where, really, have I ever been?

A bus ride and then another tram ride took him to the road where Tom Banbury lived. A quiet suburban road with rose-bushes in the front gardens behind the laurel bushes.

Tom had the roses, unkempt, and the laurel hedge, uncut. John Coffin had never been there before, and would probably never go there again, but it was about what he had expected. It'd been a proper home once but never would be again. Not with Tom in it.

He didn't know that Tom Banbury was at home but he guessed it. There was a look to the house as if a sour, silent presence sat inside it. And he knew what created the impression: nothing psychic or anything like that, a straight physical effect. The curtains were drawn back, but unhandily so that no window matched, while a lean, long-nosed tabby cat sat on the doorstep, mouthing silently.

Tom Banbury opened the door himself. He surveyed Coffin without a word. Without surprise, either.

'Come on in then, Moses.' He opened the door wider, the cat entered, followed by Coffin.

'Moses?' Funny name for a cat. 'Why do you call him Moses?'

'Seemed to suit him.'

It was true the cat did have a cool, legalistic look as if he might be a great law-giver. The nose for it, you might say.

Banbury was drinking. Not whisky as yet but a mug of tea. He put down a plate of fish for Moses, a large cod's head with dull eye stared up from the dish.

'Have some tea.' It was a statement not a question. He poured a dark stream from a pot with a broken spout, depositing a spatter of dark stains to join others on the table.

Coffin hugged the mug to him, not wanting to drink with Tom Banbury. He needed to get the conversation over first. It takes a funny sort of a man to shop a mate.

'Drink up.' He made it an order.

Coffin took a sip: so that was where the whisky was.

'Don't fancy it? Don't you like whisky?'

'It's not that, sir.'

'But you don't think it's right to be drinking my whisky?'

This was so nearly true that Coffin was silenced.

'I suppose you don't remember what today is?'

More than a tipple from the brown pot, thought Coffin; emotion as well.

'It's the day the jury will decide that Ned Summers is guilty of killing Connie Shepherd. In the statutory time he will be hanged.'

'Oh, that. Yes, I did know.'

'And you're not thinking about it? You ought to be thinking about it.'

'I am, sir. In a way. I think he asked for it and he got it. We did our job.' He added deliberately, 'I think there was an over-reaction to the Shepherd murder. I guess you noticed it yourself, I *thought* I noticed it. And I'd say a report went to Dander. Right at the beginning, that would be. Perhaps there had already been a note that this chap got worked up in a way he shouldn't.' But it was not only because of Summers, it was the girl's body.

'How old are you, Detective-Constable Coffin?'

'Twenty-two, sir.' And you know, sir.

There was silence. Banbury put his mug down with a bang. 'Come on, then. Out with it. What you came to say.'

Coffin got his speech into some sort of shape. Perhaps the whisky helped it all out.

'There's a question of loyalties, see.' The native Londoner was showing through his speech more and more, the little Cockney fighting to get out. 'Someone you got to know in the army, saw things through with: Vic Padovani.'

'So you feel loyal to him?'

'Like him.' The reply was dogged. 'Don't want to see him go down for murders he did not do.'

Tom Banbury was silent. 'You think so? He's done other things.'

'Yes. Dealt in black-market shoes and fake wine. He always did do that kind of deal. I knew that in the army. It's the way the Padovanis live.'

'So?'

'That's one loyalty, but then there's another kind. Loyalty to what I am now, loyalty to someone I've worked with. Got to like.'

'Oh, you have, have you?'

Tom Banbury laughed. It was a kind laugh, no threat in it as with some laughs, but almost without humour. A laugh like a full stop. Then he pushed the teapot Coffin's way again. 'It's a bugger, isn't it? Drink up. If it's any comfort to you, I know what you know.'

'I thought you might.'

'Vic Padovani didn't kill those women. Not the type. I know it and now you know it.' He stood up. 'How long?'

'Almost from the beginning. When I saw the first body, saw the card with the stain. Reminded me of something. I know I was on the edge of everything.

Thought nothing of it at first, then I thought, no, it's deliberate. Policy.'

'That's right.' 'Other duties. Segregation as if we had an infectious disease. Well, I knew I didn't have it, so I had to work out who had. I thought I could make out a picture. Of course I knew Warwick and Dander must have put together a dossier, full of details that I didn't know. But I thought I had something they didn't have. I was close. And I saw someone who had shown a strong reaction to the murder of Connie Shepherd, more than I would have expected. Perhaps been obsessed by it. Particularly in relation to the child. I thought the child-mother relation was crucial. That was where Rachel Esthart came in.'

Tom Banbury did not answer.

'But although it looked as if she was the centre, I don't think she was.

'It seemed to me that the murderer hated women who were unmaternal. Perhaps he had a personal reason for hating them. Perhaps his own mother had ill-treated him. Or rejected him. He might have been an orphan. Or unloved.'

'Go on.'

'He went for three women who rejected children, so perhaps he was punishing them. That was how I thought. Lorna Beezley didn't like the children she taught. Every one seemed to know. Shirley Cowley complained bitterly about family responsibilities. Eileen Gaze left her child at every possible opportunity. She wasn't a loving mother.'

'You've got some interesting ideas, there.'

'We were all fussing around Rachel Esthart on account of the letter. So it looked as if the origin to it all must lie in her past. Not so.'

'No?'

'Oh, she was hated all right. And for the same reason the other women were killed; because she had abandoned her child. But the *first* victim did not have a card. She died before that started.

'So the killings started *after* the death of Connie Shepherd, but *before* Rachel Esthart got her letter. Connie Shepherd was the clue, not Rachel. Mrs Esthart was a bit of embroidery that came later. It was a way of making her suffer, killing her in another way. I should think the killer enjoyed it.'

'I believe he may have done, son.'

'But she wasn't crucial. She thought she was, but she was really unimportant. He may have liked that too. Dragging her down.'

'He did.'

'So I was looking for a killer, who had, as I had seen for myself, reacted strongly, even unnaturally to the death of Connie Shepherd; who hated women because of his own family background, who probably hated sexual relations. A man who had and knew how to use a knife. A man who knew the theatre crowd, who knew The Padovani, and who knew Rachel Esthart. Right?'

'I don't reject the picture. It's got a lot of truth in it.'

'The killer was someone I knew. Someone I worked with. That was what I came to see, that was where loyalty came in.' He had known from the moment that the killer spoke of the card in Shirley's brassière, he should not have known. 'I might have stayed quiet. Only might. But poor old Vic. Couldn't let him go down without a try.'

The words had come tumbling out. The murderous sequence of events, established bit by bit in his mind, had to be displayed to Banbury. He was a man he had to tell. It seemed only right. Loyalty went that far.

Connie Shepherd was the precipitating factor. Her murder set the killer off, finally pushed him into a violence that his own childhood, and then the war, had prepared him for. He was not a man who should have chosen the job he had. Or should have been weeded out. Connie Shepherd had died. The killer had probably not sought out Eileen Gaze, and perhaps not even understood then what he was looking for. But once found he had known what to do.

He had known how to ingratiate himself (poor old Vic and his black-market shoes), to get on easy terms. But having killed once, then he went out looking for victims to hate, to mutilate and kill. Thus Lorna Beezley and Shirley Cowley, not picked on arbitrarily but chosen, definitely chosen.

What turned a policeman into a killer? Or did he become a policeman because he was attracted to what he feared?

Tom Banbury said deliberately, 'What you know, and what I know, you can bet Dander and Warwick know. Suspected quite a while, I'd say. Dander's a sharp one. That was why we were all set carefully aside while they worked it all out. Had to be sure, you see. Loyalty again.'

Coffin said: 'One thing this man—'

'Whom you haven't named.'

'Whom I haven't named. This man, the killer living in a fantasy world, wouldn't he try to create his own reality by keeping a record? Writing down *his* truth?'

There was a silence.

'Yes. Clever boy.' Tom Banbury opened a drawer, he produced a neat, stapled-together clutch of papers which he held for a moment in his hand, then offered silently to John Coffin.

Coffin took them. 'Typed?'

'You wouldn't expect it to be handwritten. Typed on my own office typewriter.'

'And?'

'Taped beneath a drawer in the office. Safe enough till the painters came in today and dislodged them moving the furniture and handed them to me. Not a bad place to keep them if you think of the psychology of policemen.'

And wanted to take the mickey out of them, thought Coffin. Policemen usually keep their own kennel clean.

He read through the pages quickly. It was all there: the names of the victim, dates, and details. One blank page at the end. He didn't like that.

Banbury said, 'Did you speak to anyone about all this before you set out?'

'I left a note or two around,' said Coffin awkwardly. 'You know what I mean? I had a feeling Dander and Warwick were moving in.' There had been rumours flying around the station all day. 'So I did that, then came on here to talk to you.'

'You silly young fool, you've really stuck your neck out.' Banbury sounded almost sympathetic, as if, had the situation been otherwise, he would have done the same.

Memories of the seagull pinned to the door of Angel House were flooding back, bringing panic with them. Coffin had been wrong to dismiss all that as icing on the cake! The bird had meant something after all, and Stella had known it. Wasn't she the seagull?

Tom Banbury drew breath. 'You bloody fool.' Then he relented. 'You young, bloody fool.'

STELLA'S BODY LAY spreadeagled on the ground. Her eyes were wide open so that she could see the sky, she could hear the ships on the river. What she felt was the murderer's hands on her neck.

'You'll be the exception. Not in the river, but you were too good to miss, Stella. And I've had you on my mind all along, little bird.'

'Why me?' she managed to gasp. Keep talking, Stella, she told herself.

'You instead of Rachel Esthart. She's too old, but if I kill you I will kill her child again for her. She'll hate that or love it, who knows?'

Stella whispered, 'Please don't, Alex.'

'I've known about her since I was a kid. Saw her once, and she saw me. Never told her that. My father, my *own* father Charley King, not the bastard who became my stepfather and made me take his name, was a copper in Oxfordshire where the kid drowned. I was not understood. Do you understand that? *I was not understood.*' He was shouting. Then his voice dropped. 'I saw the drowned boy—never forgot it. Every time I saw a body in the war I saw the kid beside it. Not really, I'm not mad. But it certainly made me interested in putrefaction.' He gave Stella a shake. 'You next.' It was a hard, cruel movement, full of violence to come. 'I found the letter in which you named me as a man you feared. Clever, but silly, Stella, to name names.' In his pocket was Stella's letter; the powdering of rust which had fallen inside it had rested upon his name, staining it. 'And even if you are Rachel's substitute, my little seagull, you count on your own because you are as bad as those other bitches. They hated children, I heard them say so. That's why I chose them. They were not fit to go on living.'

'I am, please,' whispered Stella. 'Let me live. And you will be caught. I wrote your name on another letter.'

'No, you didn't, little seagull. I don't believe you. I can tell truth from lies. I cannot be stopped. Cannot. I am invulnerable. I will never be caught. The only thing that might point to me were the shoes which I got for Lorna, Shirley and Eileen. *That* was why they went out with me. I got them from Vic, but who's going to believe him now? No. It is evidence against Vic as a killer. A bit of luck for me.' He tightened his grip on her. 'Anyway, who believes in luck? Not me. I plan. If I am caught I shall be punished. And I shall deserve to be punished. But I won't get caught. There's a ship sailing tonight on the high tide from the King William Dock. High tide is an hour from now. I'll be on her. When she docks in Liverpool I'll melt away. Who finds anyone in Liverpool? I might start again there.'

Stella knew what he meant by 'start again'. Would there be no end? She moved a little, trying to get her neck free. 'Let me go. Please.'

'To tell you the truth, I never believed I was Charley King's son, either. I knew I didn't belong in *that* set-up. I had a fantasy I was really Rachel Esthart's lost son. That lasted a long while, longer than you'd think, even though I knew it wasn't true. I was going to be her son and a ballet-dancer. I used to masturbate and think about it.'

Stella gave a moan, speedily repressed by the killer with rough hands.

'By that time Charley King was dead and I'd had my name changed by my stepfather; I hated him, but I hated my mother more for abandoning me. That's what she'd done. I don't think she even liked me: she said I was a difficult birth. A mean, lying, peevish, selfish woman, just like those others. Like Rachel Esthart. Like you would be if you got the chance. You *are* her, a monster in the making, fit to be killed.'

As he pressed against her, she felt the knife in his hands: a small, squat weapon, sharpened by his honing.

Bloody Boy Scout, thought Stella. A fierce anger gave her a surge of strength. She dragged at his hands, trying to free her throat.

In the bushes that grow on the hill by the Royal Observatory, just above where Alex Rowley had taken Stella, crouched a small figure.

Paul Shanks, no longer the intrepid Eagle Scott, was a frightened little boy. But a brave one.

He began to shout as he ran forward, just as Stella began to scream.

Coffin would have liked to have been the one to rescue Stella and lay his hands on Alex Rowley, but that pleasure was denied him.

The honour went jointly to Paul Shanks and Albert Jones, lighterman, exercising his pregnant bullterrier bitch, Patsy, in Greenwich Park.

Come to think of it, perhaps Patsy did the best job. Her jaws fixed themselves firmly in Alex Rowley's arm.

THAT WET SUMMER of 1946 came into its full flower.

The King and Queen together with the two princesses made a triumphant tour through the bombed streets of South London. They paused to take tea at Greenwich and to watch the entire cast of the Theatre Royal, Nelson Street, perform their Masque. Stella was a delight as the Virgin, while Bluebell charmed everyone as her attendant nymph, one pretty shoulder bare. Chris Mackenzie's music could hardly be heard in the open air for the sounds of river and traffic, but a notable patron was there and *did* hear enough to commission a mass for the music festival he was about to launch in Windsor.

The real triumph was Rachel's. As her price for financial rescue of Joan and Albie's repertory company, she took the part of The Virgin Queen away from poor Joan.

RACHEL ESTHART RESURGENT, ran the headlines in *The Times*. The *Kentish Mercury* had a full page of pictures, together with a special interview from Rachel who radiantly declared her intention of returning to the theatre. It was what she had been planning. Now Stella knew, she could only admire her skill.

Paul Shanks delivered his paper in person. He was wearing his gold watch, a joint present from Rachel and Stella. He was accompanied by a small bull-terrier puppy called Stella.

'You had to see the joke,' said Stella to John Coffin. 'That boy will go far, damn him.' She took his hand. 'I'm going far, darling, too.'

They ate at The Padovani restaurant where one of the girls served them. Vic and his papa were serving a sentence for their black-market dealings. The beetroot wine which had stained the cards sent out by Alex was still mysteriously on sale. It had a different name but the flavour was all its own.

'With Chris,' he said bitterly.

'As to that, darling, who can say?' Who could, with Stella? 'But I've had an offer, solid, from a London management. A star part; Albie is releasing me. I'll be off, darling. But I do love you. Always will, in a way, my way.'

Tears of regret welled up in her lovely eyes.

Arms around each other, they walked back to Angel House. Coffin still lived at Mrs Lorimer's; you couldn't desert the old bird. He still hadn't met Lady Olivia, though, but she had been quieter.

He was very unhappy inside at what he'd done to Alex. The trial would come up soon. Then that condemned cell business. He understood Tom Banbury on that matter a bit better now. There has to be a hangman, of course, but you didn't have to like it. Tom Banbury had gone to Aberdeen, where he believed he had evidence about Sybil Shepherd. He turned out to be right. A couple there had the child in their care. They also had a story of befriending a runaway lost child, of wanting to keep her. It sounded true. But the main thing was the girl herself was safe and well. She might even have found herself a home.

'What about you?'

'Me?' I have made an ally, a patron, of Chief Superintendent Dander, I have not exactly endeared myself to Inspector Warwick, and I really like Tom Banbury, God bless his brown teapot. 'I'm doing all right.' In my pocket I have a small cyanide capsule which I liberated in Germany from a Gestapo officer, who lost his nerve. I might slip it to Alex if I get *my* nerve. He saw himself there, in the condemned cell,

trying to talk, and Alex as silent ever. No expression
on his face as he palmed the capsule. 'Did I tell you I
called at that house in Charlton? The old chap there
said no, it wasn't him that adopted a child, but his
senior butcher; a man called Carver. Carver bought a
shop of his own in Deptford in 1936. He gave me the
address. He knows there *was* a child.' Coffin gave
Stella a regretful smile. 'But he can't remember the
sex, boy or girl, he doesn't know.'

Still he was a step closer to finding his sibling. He
would be trying to find the Carver shop in Deptford,
but he had certain clues. Wasn't he the detective? He
looked forward into his future, dimly foreseeing that
it would be filled with monotonous, dirty, exhausting
tasks and days of drudgery in which he would be in
turn psychologist, pathologist, lawyer and humble
searcher after truth. In short: a policeman. But he
looked forward with hope: to him it seemed golden.

'Goodbye, Stella.'

Because it was goodbye. He watched her go into
Angel House.

'Keep in touch.' Would he ever see her again? The
wind picked up his voice and carried it down river and
out to sea.

ALEX ROWLEY, whose surname had provoked his
stepfather Bob Rowley's only known joke (Alex's own
father was called Charley King; King Charles II was
nicknamed Old Rowley; in making Alex call himself
Rowley, Bob had mockingly given him a version of his
name. He thought it Funny), did not take the cyanide

pill, and died by hanging, as enigmatic as he had lived (Liverpool never knew what it had missed) on November 30, 1946.

It was a difficult death.

Under the INFLUENCE

A BEN & CARRIE PORTER MYSTERY

ELIZABETH TRAVIS

First Time in Paperback

Gorgeous and charming, the talented artist was simply irresistible—even to happily married women like Carrie Porter. But when the egocentric playboy is found shot dead and stabbed in an office at Carrie and Ben Porter's publishing firm, it's clear somebody had had enough of Greg and his mating games.

Ben and Carrie are drawn into the sordid underbelly of raging passions and devious manipulation—and unveil a bloody portrait of a murder.

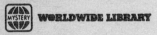

THIS BLESSED PLOT

M.R.D. MEEK
A LENNOX KEMP MYSTERY

Rich and poor. Lennox Kemp knew they all had their peculiarities. On the other side of the tracks—although disguised behind fine crystal and patrician smiles—were the Courtenays.

Twins Vivian and Venetia were rich, reckless and probably quite ruthless. They needed Kemp to oversee the legalities of the rather bizarre plans for their massive inheritance....

"M.R.D. Meek moves ever closer to the charmed company of Ruth Rendell and P. D. James."
—*Detroit News*

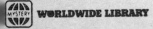

BARBARA PAUL
IN-LAWS
and
OUTLAWS

Gillian Clifford, once a Decker in-law, returns to the family fold to comfort Raymond's widow, Connie. Clearly, the family is worried. Who hates the Deckers enough to kill them?

And as the truth behind the murder becomes shockingly clear, Gillian realizes that once a Decker, always a Decker—a position she's discovering can be most precarious indeed.

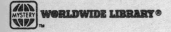